Deveron Hall

Deveron Hall

VELDA JOHNSTON

A Novel of Suspense

DODD, MEAD & COMPANY
New York

For my cousin, Esther Harris Lackland

Deveron Hall

Chapter
One

Sheep were blocking my way again. As I had learned during the drive north from Glasgow, sheep rule the road in Scotland. The beam of my headlights, which had grown brighter as the long summer twilight deepened, shone on fat, twitching white tails, on black faces that turned to stare blandly at my secondhand—or perhaps fourth- or-fifth-hand —Toyota. I inched the little car forward. Taking their time about it, the bleating creatures ambled off into the shallow ditches at either side of the narrow dirt road.

Ahead was a wooden bridge spanning a stream. And about a mile beyond it, according to the barmaid back there at the pub in the tiny village of Harlaig, was the long private drive which would lead me up Deveron Hall.

Ten minutes before, when I had entered the pub and said good evening to the middle-aged woman behind the bar, I had been aware of only casual interest in the faces of the men and women seated at the small tables or moving about with ale mugs in hand. In July American visitors, even unaccompanied young women, apparently were no novelty here in the Highlands. But when I asked the distance to Deveron Hall, the cozy little room with its flocked red wallpaper suddenly became silent.

A hope, never strong, had died within me—the hope that Marcia Deveron had been able to return to her native region unobtrusively and settle down among people whose memory of her had grown dim. The silence in the amber-lighted pub parlor, only a moment before filled with talk and laughter and the thud of darts against the target board, told me that they remembered only too well.

Did they remember, also, that Marcia Deveron was the mother of a daughter? Perhaps not. Eighteen years ago, at the time of her trial for murder here in Scotland, I had been a seven-year-old, left behind with my paternal grandparents in southern California.

I thanked the barmaid. As I hurried through that silence toward the door, I saw a man seated alone at a table. He was thirty or a bit more, with a strong-featured face, dark blond hair, and gray eyes that looked at me, not just with curiosity, but with an alertness which, it seemed to me, was touched with alarm.

Outside I saw that the almost full moon, only a pale circle half an hour ago, was brighter now. I was about to get into my car when I heard footsteps on the gravel behind me. When I turned around the blond man said, "Forgive me, but I felt I should warn you about the bridge."

If he was one of the locals, obviously he belonged to the gentry. His accent bore no resemblance to the barmaid's Scottish burr. Instead it was that of a man educated at one of those expensive private establishments which the British insist upon calling public schools.

"The bridge?"

"Over the stream. It is badly in need of repair. If you try to go over it fast, you may bounce into the guardrail."

I gave him the level look his flimsy excuse for approaching me deserved. Why should anyone, especially a stranger to this region, drive fast over a dirt road only a car-length wide and, moreover, clogged with sheep every few hundred yards? "Thank you," I said.

"Not at all." After a moment he added, "My name is Michael MacKelvin."

MacKelvin. Someone of that name had figured in the newspaper accounts of my mother's arrest. Had it been one of the guests at that house party at Deveron Hall? If so, he must have been some other MacKelvin. This man, surely, had been in his early teens eighteen years ago.

Obviously he was waiting for me to give my name. Tired from the long day's drive in an alien country, and taut with both anticipation and dread of meeting a mother of whom I had only childhood memories, I had no intention of revealing to this alert-eyed stranger that I was Craig Marsden and Marcia Deveron's daughter.

I said, "Thank you again, Mr. MacKelvin. And good night." Without another glance at him, I got into the Toyota, drove off the graveled parking space onto the road, and turned left.

Now, as I moved over the bridge above the foaming stream, I found that its surface was somewhat rough. But no one used to the potholed streets of Manhattan and Brooklyn would have considered the bridge "badly in need of repair."

I drove on. There ahead on the right, almost at the top of the gently rising eastern wall of this valley, stood the dark shape of a house. My pulse leaped. Deveron Hall? Yes, it must be, for here was the turnoff.

I moved up the long narrow drive between rows of tall pines, black in the moonlight, that my grandfather, or perhaps even my great-grandfather, must have planted years ago on this otherwise treeless hillside. As I drew closer, I saw that the house, of some dark-colored stone, was about what I had expected from those old newspaper pictures—no ancient and stately pile, but the sort of solid, comfortable house that successful Scottish businessmen of the nineteenth century, deciding to abandon trade for the more gentlemanly vocation of sheep farming, had built for themselves in the Highlands.

Not for the first time these past two days, I wondered why my mother, once she was free and able to go anywhere she chose, had come to this house. As far as I could see, there could be only one explanation. Like a distraught and wounded animal hurrying to its lair, she had returned to the house where she had been born.

But I could not conceive of her fleeing here, no matter how distraught, unless she had been innocent of that terrible crime for which she had stood trial. Not just innocent in terms of the jury's verdict—"not guilty by reason of insanity" —but actually innocent. All through the years of my growing up, I had clung to the belief—a belief I had hidden from my father's parents—that my mother had not killed Craig Marsden. It was someone else who, on a summer night long ago in that house up ahead, had entered my father's study and, under cover of the noisy party in progress across the hall, had stabbed him repeatedly until he died.

I could see the house in more detail now, there on its level space just below the hillside's brow. It was of Georgian style, with a semicircular portico supported by pillars, white and gleaming in the moonlight. At the left of the portico, lamplight filtered through a crack in draperies drawn across a first-floor window to reveal a bed of what looked like bright red geraniums. My mother, who had been here only a few weeks, could not have planted those flowers. Perhaps, in anticipation of her release, a gardener had been hired by the trustees who, these past eighteen years, had been responsible for the house and its several hundred acres of valley and moorland, as well as the rest of my mother's estate.

I became aware that my mouth had become dry, and my pulse faint and rapid. What would my mother look like now? Was she still beautiful? I remembered her leaning over my bed to kiss me good night, a glorious green-eyed creature with red-gold curls piled atop her head, and with bare shoulders gleaming above a strapless green evening dress. I remembered sitting on a Hollywood sound stage, legs dangling from a canvas chair, while on the brightly lighted set, which had represented the front wall and terrace of a big white frame house, a makeup man fussed around my mother, dabbing ocher powder on her chin, and tucking a stray red-gold curl into place. The memory also included a sense of my father up there somewhere in the shadowy reaches of the sound stage, seated beside the cameraman on the gigantic camera boom. Although I of course did not realize it at the time, I was a completely happy child that day, pleased by the flattering attention of the crew and other members of the cast, and proud that I was the only little girl in the world with movie star Marcia Deveron for a mother and director Craig Marsden for a father.

I prayed that she had not changed too much. But no matter what she was like now, I would stay here the whole summer, if she would let me. Perhaps I would stay even longer, if I found out that I could get a job in some school here in Scotland.

A few yards from the house, another drive struck off to the right from the main one, apparently leading back to a garage. I turned left and stopped the Toyota in front of the portico. As I started up the shallow steps, light bloomed in the hall behind the tall doors of frosted glass. Then the light in the portico ceiling came on. She opened the doors and stood there on the threshold, a thin little figure in black pants and a black turtleneck sweater.

Chapter Two

My heart seemed to contract with disappointment and shocked pity. No, my mother was no longer beautiful. Only the green eyes and the red-gold hair, worn almost shoulder-length, reminded me of the lovely creature I had adored. And the portico light was bright enough to reveal that her hair was dyed. What was it like, really? Faded and gray-streaked? Or even whiter than her thin face with its lines bracketing the mouth, lines that deepened as she gave me a tentative smile? True, she was still in her forties, but after eighteen years' confinement in that place her hair might well have turned the snowy white of great age.

She said in a strained voice, "Lisa?"

I stretched my lips into a smile. "Yes, I'm Lisa."

How bleakly different this moment was from what I had hoped. I had pictured us hurling ourselves, tearful with joy, into each other's arms. And here we stood, speaking in voices as stiff as our smiles.

She moved aside. "Won't—won't you come in?"

When I stood beside her in the wide, oak-paneled hall, I realized how short she was, not more than five-feet-one-or-two to my five-feet-six. That too was a shock. True, the old fan magazines I had read surreptitiously during my adolescence had often referred to her as "petite." But somehow I had expected her to be as tall as she had appeared in my young-child's eyes.

She said, "You look so much like—" Abruptly she broke off.

"Yes," I said. My father had been tall and, like me, he'd had dark hair and blue eyes.

An awkward silence lengthened. Then she made a tentative gesture toward me. I bent and kissed her. Her lips were cool and dry.

"Do you want to come into the study? I built a fire in there. I know it's July now. But I felt—chilled."

We moved through a doorway. Firelight and lamplight gleamed on tall bookshelves, on a mahogany desk with a green-shaded lamp, on dark red draperies. Those at glass doors on one side of the room had been drawn back, so that the room's light fell on a brick terrace beyond. Chairs of dark brown leather were drawn up on either side of the hearth. When we had sat down, my mother took a brass-handled poker from its metal stand and prodded the smoldering fire log into a blaze.

I asked unnecessarily, "Did you get my wire?" The wire I had sent from Glasgow that morning, afraid that if I telephoned her she would protest my coming here.

"Yes." She kept her gaze on the fire log.

Again strained silence settled down. I looked around the room, and then stiffened with realization. This must be the room where my father had died. How could she bear to be here, only a few feet away from the desk across which he had sat slumped, bleeding from knife wounds in his back and throat?

But then at her trial, according to the accounts in those old newspapers, she had testified that she had no memory of even being in this room that long-ago summer night. She remembered mingling with her house party guests in the big drawing room of this now-silent house. Then, abruptly, she found herself in her upstairs bedroom, with drying blood on her hands, and more blood stiffening the front of her white dress, and with stricken-faced friends hovering around her bed, and the tramping feet of just-arrived police loud in the downstairs hall.

Now the fact that she could sit here in this room seemed to me further proof of her innocence. If she had stabbed my father, even in a moment of mental aberration, she would not be able to sit in this room. Her instincts—the gentle, loving instincts of the woman who had been the center of my universe for my first seven years of life—would have forbidden her to do so.

I asked, "Did you get my last letter?"

I meant the letter I had written two months ago, after I had received word from the chief of staff of that asylum outside London that my mother soon would be released. In my letter I had told her that I wanted to come to her.

"Yes, I got it."

I wanted to say, "Then why didn't you answer? Why didn't you ever answer any of my letters?" But these past two days, as I drove north from London, I had kept warning myself not to pressure her, or reproach her, or upset her in any way. I wanted to heal her, if I could, not subject her to the sort of emotional stress that might hurl her back into the place she had just left.

She answered my unspoken question. "I never wrote to you because I—I didn't want you to come to me, and I didn't know just how to tell you that. I mean, you're young, and you've got your work, and a whole life separate from mine—" She broke off. "You didn't quit your job to come here, did you?"

My teaching job, in the fourth grade of a Brooklyn public school. "No. School isn't in session during the summers."

"Of course. It's been so long— I mean, I'd forgotten that."

I said, "I would have come to London long ago to see you, except that—" Appalled, I stopped speaking. Fatigue and strain must have rendered me stupid. I had almost spoken of the bitterness toward her that her parents-in-law— my grandparents and legal guardians—had never been able to overcome.

"Except," I said lamely, "that I was afraid seeing me might not be good for you."

She nodded, gaze fixed on the thin hands clasped in her lap.

Everything, I realized wretchedly, was going all wrong. It was not just that she seemed withdrawn and apathetic. I too felt an emotional numbness. True, her altered appearance had been a shock. But it was shameful that something she could not help should make me feel alienated, rather than even more tender and protective.

I said, "You know my grandparents were killed in a plane crash a few months ago, don't you? I wrote to you about it right after it happened."

I had known it was safe to write to her about it. The hospital staff, who screened incoming mail, would not have allowed her to receive any news they considered possibly harmful.

She nodded. "I remember."

"And that means I'm all alone in the world now, just as you are. I thought that the two of us—"

"But you mustn't think of me as alone." The green eyes lifted to my face. "Amy is here. My cousin, Amy Deveron. Only it is Amy Harnish now. She's been married and divorced."

I said incredulously, "You mean, she's living here?"

"Yes. She's in her room now. She goes to bed early. You see, she isn't well. Her heart isn't strong, and she's got something wrong with her eyes. I forget the name of it."

"Glaucoma?"

"That's it."

"Where was she living before she came here? London?"

My mother nodded.

From my search of the back files of *The New York Times* I knew quite a lot about Amy Deveron. The prosecutor at the trial had claimed that Amy—or, rather, Amy's attractiveness to my father—had been the motive for my mother's act. Learning of the affair between her husband and her cousin, the prosecutor contended, she had attacked him in a jealous frenzy.

And now here were the two women, living together in the house where, eighteen years before, the man that perhaps both of them had loved had met his violent death.

She said, as if aware of my bewildered astonishment, "What happened here was all so long ago. And Amy was very good to me while I was in—that place. She came to see me as often as she could."

I wondered why. Affection? Pity? Some sort of guilt?

"Besides," she went on, "Amy's had a hard time. Her marriage was absolutely wretched. And anyway, she and I grew up together in this house. We were more like sisters than cousins."

I said nothing. I did not want her to know how assiduously I had researched that old murder case, reading through a viewer microfilmed copies of newspapers and magazines until my eyes burned and my head ached. And so I did not tell that I already knew about her childhood association with her year-younger cousin, Amy Deveron.

My grandfather, David Deveron, had been the elder of my great-grandfather's two sons, and thus the sole inheritor of his house and lands. But after his younger brother died, leaving a motherless nine-year-old daughter, David Deveron had brought his niece here to raise with his own daughter.

I thought of the two girls growing up in this house at the moor's edge, with its view of the valley below. According to an article I had read in an old copy of *Time*, from childhood on Amy as well as my mother had wanted to become an actress. Both of them as young teen-agers had appeared in Shakespearean plays staged by the Mayberry School for Girls near the village of Harlaig. Perhaps, too, they acted out bits from movies they must have seen during visits to the nearest sizable town, Inverness—Cathy and Heathcliff wandering the moors, or Joan Crawford bullying her maid in *Craig's Wife*.

There must have been a strong affection between them, at least on my mother's side. At the age of eighteen, when she won a place in the cast of a London repertory company, she managed to have her cousin assigned to minor roles. When she was offered a Hollywood contract, she tried without success to obtain a contract for Amy. In Hollywood, after she married the man who became my father, she tried to get him to send for her cousin and see to it that some studio signed her. My father, quite understandably, had refused to take a chance on an actress whose work he had never seen. It was not until Marcia Deveron and Craig Marsden came to London to make a movie that the two cousins were re-united.

My mother was staring at the fire again. I said, "Are just the two of you here? I mean, do you have live-in servants?"

She turned her face toward me with a jerky movement, as if she had forgotten my presence. "No. Just a girl, Jennie

Graham, who comes in early in the morning and leaves after dinner."

There had been a John and Flora Graham, gardener and housekeeper, at Deveron Hall that summer of my father's death. They had testified for the prosecution at my mother's trial. I wondered if this Jennie Graham was a relation.

My mother went on, "The—the trustees tried to get some couple from the village to live in here, but no one would do it."

No, I thought, most servants would not want to sleep beneath the roof of a woman, recently released from a mental hospital, who had been adjudged the murderer of her husband.

She said, "Did you ask about servants because—I mean, I never thought. Perhaps you're hungry. I could fix—"

"No, no! I had dinner in Inverness. I just meant that if you had no one here except Amy Harnish, a woman who isn't well—"

"But I do have someone else. Richard Coventry is staying here. He drove Amy and me up from London."

For the first time, animation had come in her voice. "Richard Coventry?" I asked. "Who is—"

"A—a very good friend of mine. He went to Inverness on business this afternoon. He should be back soon."

I felt dismay. To judge by the tone of her voice and the faint smile curving her lips, she was smitten with this Richard Coventry, whoever he was. It was a state that might be perilous indeed for a frail woman newly emerged from an asylum.

"Have you known him long?"

"In a way. I met him when I came to London to make *The Thorn Tree.*"

The film she and my father had made that summer eighteen years before.

"But it's just lately that I got to know him well." With that little smile still on her lips, she had returned her gaze to the fire. "After—after I was released, Amy took me to a London hotel for a few days, and Richard looked me up there."

And so, apparently, he had not been to see her during all her years in the hospital. "Is he in the movie business?"

"He used to be an actor. But he's in real estate now."

Real estate. The Deveron property represented quite a lot of real estate, hundreds of acres that could be re-stocked with sheep, or serve as a private hunting preserve for rich men who came in ever-increasing numbers from England and the continent to shoot grouse.

She added, "Richard is my fiancé."

After a stunned moment I said, "I see."

I too looked at the fire, afraid that she might read my thoughts in my eyes. What sort of man must Richard Coventry be? Well, possibly he could be a man who fell in love with her all those years ago, stood helplessly by while she was tried for murder, and then waited patiently—for some reason not even trying to see her—until she was released from the hospital.

Yes, that was possible. Almost anything was possible. But more probably he was a man taking advantage of a frail, confused, and fairly rich woman.

She was looking at me now. "And so, Lisa, you see that you don't have to worry about me. And you don't have to stay here. I'll be all right."

"It's not a case of *having* to—"

I broke off. What was wrong with me? Why couldn't I try to break down this strange barrier between us by saying the warm, tender things that I had expected to say, things that she must be wanting me to say? Because despite her surface withdrawnness, she too must be remembering our mother-and-young-daughter closeness—our frolics in the pool of the Beverly Hills house, and the times we sat on the terrace beside it, she in a canvas chair with a blue-covered script in her hands, I stretched out on my stomach on the flagstones, turning the pages of a picture book.

Was she remembering, too, the times my handsome father had taken us both to lunch at the Brown Derby, or given us skiing lessons up at Big Bear? Perhaps not. Perhaps she had learned how to suppress memories of the man everyone, probably including herself, believed she had killed.

She gave me that strained little smile. "All right. If you really want to stay, then I want you to, for as long as you like."

Guiltily, I realized that I felt tempted not to stay here in this isolated house with its memories of tragedy and violence. I had an impulse to flee from the white-faced woman opposite me, and that other woman invisible somewhere upstairs, and the "fiancé" who at any moment might walk into this dimly lighted room. If I left for London tomorrow morning, I might be back in New York in not much more than forty-eight hours from now. Back in my pleasant apartment on the top floor of an old Brooklyn Heights brownstone, with the river and the towers of Manhattan beyond visible from its front window. Back with my bright young friends, including the several attractive men I dated, and one of whom I might marry.

But to leave would have been both cowardly and selfish. Despite Amy Deveron Harnish and Richard Coventry, she needed me, this broken woman who had given me life. In fact, it could be that their presence—or at least the presence of Richard Coventry—made it all the more imperative that I stay here.

Besides, I loved her. It was just the numbing strangeness of this reunion that made it hard for me to express, or even feel, that love. With a stab of shame I realized that as yet I had not even called her Mother.

"I made up your room for you. Do you—" She paused, head raised in a listening attitude. "There's Richard's car."

I too could hear a car approaching up the long drive. "Did he know I was coming?"

"Yes. Your wire came before he left for Inverness."

"My car's still in front of the steps. Perhaps I should—"

"Richard will drive it back to the garage for you. He'll bring your suitcase in too." She stood up. That animated look was back in her face. "I might as well give him your car keys now."

I took the keys from my shoulder bag and handed them to her. Then I waited, hearing her go out the front door, hearing a car stop, and the murmur of her voice and a man's. Then their footsteps moved along the hall toward the study.

I got to my feet. He was beside her in the doorway now, a big man in country-gentleman tweeds with a broad, handsome face and gray-streaked brown hair. I judged him to be a few years younger than my mother, forty-five, perhaps.

"So you're Lisa." He set down my plaid suitcase and extended his hand. "Welcome to Deveron Hall."

A certain quality in his smile made me feel that he was aware of his own brashness, an outsider welcoming me to the house where my mother had been born, and my grandfather before her. I too extended my hand and then withdrew it, with a little difficulty, from his clasp.

My mother said to me, "You must be awfully tired, dear. Do you want to go to your room?"

Was she, I wondered, eager for me to go upstairs so that she and Richard Coventry could be alone? "Yes," I said, "I had a long drive today."

Her hands reached tentatively toward me. I bent, and her dry lips briefly touched my cheek. "Good night, Lisa."

"Good night, Mother."

"I'll take your suitcase up," Richard Coventry said.

I followed him up a broad, mahogany-railed stair to the second floor. Here amber lights were spaced on the paneled walls between portraits of haughty-faced men and women in eighteenth-century dress. My ancestors? I was sure they were not. Until my great-grandfather had managed to grow rich, the Deverons had been poverty-stricken Glasgow weavers.

At the last door on the right, near the head of the rear stairs, Richard Coventry set down my suitcase. "Here we are." With one hand he opened the door. His other arm went around my waist, as if to guide me into the room. I felt his hand slip lower—

I pulled away from him. "Just what do you think you're doing?"

Smiling, he raised both hands in the air, as if to demonstrate the innocence of his intent. "Now wait a minute. It was just a bit of friendliness. Can't a man be a little friendly with his own stepdaughter? Or didn't she tell you that I'm to be your new papa?"

"She told me. But if there is any more of that kind of friendliness—"

"You'll do what? Tell her? You wouldn't do that to your mother. You know she mustn't be upset." He reached inside the room and switched on the light. "So if you're to stay here," he went on, "you and I might as well be friends. Isn't that right?"

I studied his face. Was he just one of those fatuous types who think that any woman, even one they have just met, will welcome a pass? Or had there been more reason than that for his "bit of friendliness"? Perhaps he wanted me out of his way, wanted me to fear that by staying here I would cause my own mother jealous pain.

If that were the case, if he really wanted to be rid of me, then perhaps it was even more urgent that I stay here.

"Good night." I picked up my suitcase, went inside my room, and closed the door.

Chapter
Three

The room I had entered reminded me of the Lincoln Room at the White House. There was the same lofty ceiling, the same sort of bed with a huge slab of a headboard about eight feet tall. The mahogany dresser and chest of drawers were also of massive Victorian design. Windows at the eastern and southern sides of the room were hung with tarnished green-gold brocade draperies which, if not as old as the furniture, were at least decades old. A counterpane of the same material covered the bed. Through a partly opened door in one wall I could see the gleam of white bathroom tile.

Did most of the bedrooms in this house have their own bathrooms? Probably. My grandfather, enlarging by shrewd investments the estate left by my great-grandfather, had lavished many thousands on this house. Even so, there was no clothes closet, only a tall mahogany wardrobe with doors carved in an acanthus leaf design. Perhaps my grandfather had felt that wardrobes were more in keeping with the period of the house.

Weary in every muscle and nerve, I opened my suitcase, placed sweaters and underwear in the bureau, and hung in the camphor-smelling wardrobe the several skirts and pants of cotton and lightweight synthetics I had brought with me.

In the small bathroom with its plain white fixtures, I took a shower in the old claw-footed tub.

Then, wearing a nightgown and robe, I drew back the bedroom's brocade draperies. The south window, I realized, must overlook the sloping hillside, the east one the moor. Despite my fatigue and disappointment, I felt an anticipatory thrill at the thought of the morning. Tomorrow I would wander over the hillside and the moor, savoring at leisure the wild Highland beauty through which I had driven that day.

Not even my struggles with road maps and the roads themselves—often so narrow that when two cars met, one would have to park in a turnout until the other passed—nor my anxiety as to how my mother would receive me, had blotted out my awareness of this austerely lovely land. The long level stretches of purple-heathered moorland, the treeless mountains covered with bracken which changed from green to brown to purple beneath drifting cloud and changing light, the foaming burns which hurtled down hillsides to mirror-still lochs in the valleys—all that had brought me a sense of almost familiar delight, as if some ancestral memory had been stirred.

I touched the wall switch. Blue-white moonlight flooded through the south window and lay in a wide swath across the bed. For a moment I thought of closing the draperies, since it would be hard to fall asleep with that radiance falling on my face. But no. Sleep would be long in coming to me anyway, despite my tiredness.

I got into bed. How silent the night was. All that day, whenever I stopped the little car, I had heard wind stir the bracken, sometimes with only a whispering sound, other times with a high keening. But evidently the wind had died, because no sound at all came through the open window.

As I lay there in a strange bed in a strange, silent house in a strange country, weighted with the disappointment of my reunion with my mother, I was suddenly assailed with a lonely longing. Not for my busy life and my friends in New York, but for my grandparents, that gentle, tragic pair who had loved and protected me through the years of my growing up.

That summer eighteen years ago, staying with them in the modest but pleasant North Hollywood bungalow their successful son had bought for them, I at first had no knowledge of the violent tragedy in an old house six thousand miles away. I only knew that when I woke up one morning my grandparents were their normal, cheerful selves, but when I came into the house in midafternoon, after several hours of playing with my dolls under the backyard pepper tree, I found that my grandfather now had a white face and hands that trembled, and that my grandmother had fallen ill—so ill that she lay in her room with the shades drawn the rest of that day and for several days thereafter.

Then one afternoon they left me in the care of neighbors. When they returned—from my father's funeral service at Forest Lawn, although I did not know that then—my grandfather told me that he had put the house up for sale. The three of us were going to upper New York State and live in a town named Fairlawn, about a hundred miles from the town in which my grandparents had lived until they came to California.

"But we can't!" I cried. "Mommy and Daddy will come back here and find us gone."

Abruptly my grandmother got to her feet and hurried from the room. In a voice that trembled, my grandfather told me that my father had gone someplace far away, and would not be back.

"You mean's he's dead?" I don't know why I said that. Perhaps I had heard death spoken of as a terrible thing. And I knew that only something terrible could make my grandfather's voice shake and my grandmother flee from the room.

He scooped me up onto his lap and pressed my head against his chest. "Yes, Lisa. And your mother has to stay over there across the ocean for a while. But you have us. We three have each other."

I said, "Can I go outside now?"

I don't remember crying that day. I just remember walking with an odd, stiff feeling in my legs, and a roaring in my ears, out to the backyard swing hung from the pepper tree. I remember sitting there, not swinging, but scuffing red pepper berries under the sole of my shoe until they disappeared into the dust.

Perhaps my grandparents thought that in a strange little town on the other side of the continent, they could keep the truth from me almost indefinitely. But I had been enrolled in the first grade of the Fairlawn public school only a few weeks when the inevitable happened. When I was about two blocks from home one cold October afternoon, four "big girls" from the third grade suddenly surrounded me. Linking hands, they circled around me and chanted, over and over again, "Your father's dead, and your mother's crazy, *and* she killed him."

Tears of pain and rage streaming down my face, I broke through the circle of my tormentors, ran the rest of the way home, and burst into the living room. My grandmother dropped the hand towel she had been embroidering and stood up. "Darling! What is it?"

I told her. "It's not true, is it? Is it?"

She sat on the sofa and drew me down beside her. Arms around me, she said, "Yes, it's true." She told me, as gently as she could, that my mother was now in a hospital in a town called Perth, in Scotland. Because of overcrowded conditions there, she would soon be transferred to a hospital outside London, where she might stay for many years. "Lisa darling, they say that when she did what she did, she wasn't responsible."

"But she did not do it." I said the words to myself, not aloud. The beloved mother who used to sit by my small bed, singing of the sweet Afton that flowed gently between its green banks, could not have killed anyone, let alone the handsome, lighthearted man we both loved.

"You're our little girl now. You're all we have." I caught the bitter note in her voice. "We want you to try to forget, and be a happy little girl."

Young as I was, I had at least a dim understanding of what my grandmother was trying to tell me. She wanted me to forget the woman who—sane or insane—had killed her and my grandfather's brilliant and beloved son, their only child. Much as she loved me, she could not bear to have me reminding her, with my tears and my questions, of that woman shut up in an asylum on the other side of the Atlantic.

I loved my grandparents. And just as I was all they had, they were all that I had. With the kind of stoicism not uncommon in children, I decided that from now on I must keep everything secret—my love and longing for my mother, my belief that she could not have done that terrible thing, and my fierce determination that someday she and I would be reunited.

My arms tightened around my grandmother's neck. "All right, Grandma. I'll forget."

I did not forget. And in my twelfth year something happened that helped keep the memory of both my parents green. We had just moved into the second of the houses we occupied in Fairlawn. Exploring the attic our first day there, I found a cache of old magazines. Among them were several *Photoplays*, the latest dated more than a year before my parents' tragedy. Feverishly I looked through them, finding pictures of Mother in a gardening hat and with a wicker basket over her arm, of my father and mother dancing at Coconut Grove, of my parents and my plump four-year-old self afloat on rubber rafts in our swimming pool. I went down to my room, returned to the attic with scissors from my manicure set, and, alert for a step on the stairs, cut out all those photographs and their accompanying text. I hid them under the lining of one of my bureau drawers, sure that my grandmother, who never pried, would not find them.

When I was eighteen, I enrolled at NYU in Manhattan. Now there was no need to be surreptitious. I spent hours at *The New York Times* and at the Time-Life Building, reading on microfilm every scrap I could find about my mother and father, and the events of that summer when they had crossed the Atlantic to make a film.

It was after the film was finished that they decided to celebrate with a house party for some members of the cast at Deveron Hall, the house in the Highlands my mother had inherited two years earlier. I could imagine them in their flower-filled suite at the Savoy, telephoning the caretaking couple at Deveron Hall, so as to make sure that there would be rooms prepared for themselves and, later on, a half-dozen guests, including my mother's cousin, Amy, and an English-born woman journalist, who, until she had drunk herself out of a job, had been the most feared of Hollywood columnists.

I could imagine, too, how lively this now silent house must have been during that party, with men and women drifting in and out of the bedrooms on this second floor, talking and laughing and joking with that extra animation that actors display when among their own kind.

On Monday night, with the party due to break up the following morning, my father had shut himself up in the study. Hours later one of the guests, emerging from the noisy drawing room, saw that the study door stood open. He crossed the threshold and then halted, transfixed.

Inside the room my father lay slumped across the desk. My mother stood motionless beside him, both arms at her side. Blood stained the front of her dress and the blade of the letter opener she grasped in her right hand.

At her trial, the defense first tried to convince the jury that my mother had only discovered the body. In a state of shock, and not knowing that was the worst thing to do, she had withdrawn the blade from his back and then just stood there, unable to move or speak, in a stupor so profound that later she could not even remember entering the study or being led from it to her upstairs bedroom.

Someone else could have committed the crime, my mother's lawyer contended. By their own admission, several of the guests had been wandering in and out of the drawing room all evening. What was more, the study doors to the side terrace stood open that warm night. Anyone could have come in from the outside, including an embittered neighbor who once had lost a lawsuit against the Deverons.

But the defense was weak. There was no evidence that the angry neighbor had been anywhere near Deveron Hall that night. And none of the party guests had an apparent motive.

My mother, though, had a motive. The housekeeper, a Mrs. Graham, had testified that at intervals that whole weekend she had heard my father and mother in their room quarreling bitterly over Amy Deveron.

Fearful that my mother would be found guilty, the defense had switched to a plea of not guilty by reason of insanity. And that was the verdict the jury had decided upon. Not for the first time, I reflected that an outright guilty verdict might have brought her less suffering. She might have been released from a prison within a few years, instead of spending nearly a third of her lifetime shut up with the raving deluded, the dangerously paranoiac, the huddled catatonic.

I had sent a letter to that asylum soon after I enrolled at NYU, asking if it would be advisable for me to write to my mother. The chief of staff, a Dr. Crandall, had answered promptly. In his opinion, it would do no harm to write, but he doubted that I would receive answers. "Your mother, although apathetic and withdrawn, expresses herself forcibly upon one point. Since you have your grandparents, she feels that your life will be a happier one if you can think of her as already dead. Perhaps letters from you will change her mind. Let us hope so."

She replied to none of the letters I sent her while at NYU and during my subsequent three years as a teacher in a Brooklyn school. Then last March my grandparents and two of their neighbors, in a small plane piloted by the neighbors' son, had crashed to their deaths in the Adirondacks. Mingled with my grief had been a determination to go to my mother as soon as possible, now that I no longer had my grandparents' feelings to consider.

A few weeks before school closed, releasing my pupils and me for the summer, Dr. Crandall wrote that my mother was about to be discharged from the hospital. Immediately I made my plane reservation.

At London airport, after an all-night flight from New York, I phoned Dr. Crandall. In a warm, pleasant voice he told me that he had heard from my mother since her release. Three weeks ago she had phoned to say that she was leaving at once for her house in northwestern Scotland. "I tried to dissuade her, on the grounds that it was best for her to stay near the hospital, just in case she found life on the outside too difficult. But I could not order her to stay here. She is legally free to go wherever she chooses."

After that phone call I had gone to the airport hotel for a few hours of much-needed sleep. Late in the afternoon, from a used-car dealer, I had bought the Toyota for only a little more than plane or rail transportation to the western Highlands would have cost me. The next morning I had started driving north.

Now, lying here in the pool of moonlight, I reflected that if someone else had killed my father, then perhaps he or she also was dead now. If so, I was probably the only one in the world who believed my mother to be innocent. And what evidence did I have? Only the memory of a soft voice singing "Flow Gently, Sweet Afton." Only the memory of her coming into my room, fragrant with the sandalwood soap she always used, to rouse me from some childish nightmare and rock me in her arms until I fell asleep again.

At long last, weariness was overwhelming me. I turned on my side, facing away from the moonlight.

The name MacKelvin, stabbing through my drowsy thoughts, brought me back to full consciousness. Not the name of one of the house party guests. The name of the man who'd had a long-standing dispute with the Deveron family and, after Marcia Deveron's husband had appeared here, had tried to carry on the dispute with him. What had his first name been? John? No, James. James MacKelvin.

I thought of the man who had followed me from the pub. Was he the son of James MacKelvin? The chances were excellent that he was. And why had there been that worried alertness in his eyes? Why should he be alarmed because a young American woman had appeared, asking directions to Deveron Hall?

Let it go for now, I told myself. Sleep. Try to sleep.

A long time later, some slight sound awoke me. The moon had withdrawn from the south window, but still there was enough light for me to see the slender figure gliding from the room. The door clicked shut.

The faint fragrance of sandalwood soap still lingered in the air.

My throat tightened, and warm, grateful tears spilled down my cheeks. She had waited until she felt I must be asleep, and then she had come into this room to stand by my bed and look down at me, as she must have so often during the first seven years of my life.

She did not feel estranged from me by our long years of separation. She had pretended to do so because she was still convinced that I would be better off without her.

Well, it was up to me to convince her that she was wrong about that. I turned over in bed and again drifted off to sleep.

Chapter
Four

When I awoke the next morning, the hands of the wrist-watch I had placed on the mahogany stand beside my bed pointed to almost ten-thirty. No longer feeling tired, I got out of bed and crossed to the east window.

From this upstairs room I could see what looked like miles of undulant moorland stretching away to a rugged line of mountains, dark blue against a tender blue sky. Nearby the moor, green and brown with bracken and purple with heather, was strewn with boulders so dazzlingly white in the sunlight that for a moment I thought they were sheep. As far as I knew, though, sheep had not grazed on Deveron land for many years. I could recall how my mother during my childhood, answering my endless questions about her own early life in Scotland, had told me that her father had sold off the flocks almost as soon as he had inherited them.

I felt a lifting of my spirits. There it was, the land of my ancestors, waiting for me to explore it. Should I ask my mother to take a walk with me? No, best not. I knew now that in her heart she was glad I had come here. That was the important thing. Better to leave it up to her, who was by far the more emotionally crippled by our eighteen-year separation, to decide just how rapidly we would move toward a normal mother-daughter relationship.

I became aware that I was hungry, far too hungry to wait

for lunch. Perhaps some sort of buffet breakfast had been left in the dining room, wherever that was. Swiftly I dressed in a yellow sweater, brown pants, and a pair of old brown walking shoes. Then I left my room.

The hall was silent, all its doors closed. Which, I wondered, was my mother's room, and which ones had been assigned to Richard Coventry and Amy Deveron Harnish? I went down the stairs, noticing that the dark red carpet was faded in spots, and that several of the treads creaked. Evidently Deveron Hall, left untenanted these past eighteen years except for periodic visits from a hired caretaker, had become somewhat run-down.

On the lower floor I found that the door of the now-empty study stood open. The door opposite it, which I was sure led to the drawing room, was still closed. I hesitated for a moment, and then opened the door.

A vast room, beautifully paneled in fruitwood. From the coffered ceiling hung a crystal chandelier, its prisms iridescent in the sunlight streaming through the long, uncurtained windows. Rugs had been rolled up and stacked at the far side of the room, leaving the parquet floor bare. Dust sheets covered all the furniture, except for a grand piano near the center of the room. Had one of the party guests been playing the piano that night—perhaps something from Noel Coward, while in the smaller room across the hall—

A stray current of air from the open doorway must have stirred the chandelier's prisms. I heard a tinkling sound, like an echo of that long-silent piano. Feeling a faint chill down my spine, I backed away and closed the door.

I went on down the hall, past more haughty portraits of someone else's ancestors, and came to an open doorway. The dining room. Here the furniture, like that of my room, was of solid Victorian mahogany. But the long dark table held

no place settings, and no electric coffeepot or chafing dish stood on the massive sideboard.

I continued down the hall toward a green baize door. Beyond it must lie the kitchen. I had almost reached the baize door when I again halted, looking at more portraits. Because of their comparatively recent vintage, I was sure that this time they were not someone else's ancestors, but my own. If when I was very young I had ever seen photographs of my grandfather and great-grandfather, I did not remember them, and so I looked with interest at the portrait of a man of about fifty, with sparse reddish hair, greenish-hazel eyes, and the sort of muttonchop whiskers fashionable in the late nineteenth century. His son, my grandfather, had been painted when he also was in his middle years. He was clean-shaven and dark-haired and brown-eyed, but even so, the resemblance between the two men was remarkable—the same square face, the same shrewd gaze. So that was how they had looked, that successful Lowland businessman and his even more successful son. What would he have thought, that bewhiskered builder of Deveron Hall, if he had known that someday his house would appear in sensational headlines all over the world?

I pushed open the baize door. Beyond was a short hall, leading to an open doorway. I paused on the threshold of a big kitchen.

A carroty-haired girl of about nineteen sat at one end of a table covered with dark brown oilcloth, shelling peas into a colander. She turned her face toward me, a plain face covered with the freckles that often accompany that shade of hair.

Her small, light blue eyes were not friendly. Nevertheless, I smiled at her and said, "You must be Jennie. Jennie Graham, isn't it."

"That's right. And you must be Miss Marsden." She paused. "I suppose you're wanting breakfast. Didn't she tell you about breakfast?"

"Who?"

"Your mother."

I resisted the impulse to say, "Don't you mean Mrs. Marsden?"

It would not be wise for me to antagonize her by playing young-lady-of-the-manor, not when my mother was lucky to have any servant at all.

"No, she didn't tell me. I suppose she forgot."

Jennie smiled. "I wouldn't wonder. Well, I set breakfast out in the dining room at eight. At nine I clear away. But if you want to fix something for yourself, there's eggs in the fridge and dry cereal in the cupboard over the sink. Me, I've got lunch and dinner to do."

"Thank you," I said, careful to keep all irony out of my voice. "Cereal will be fine."

"There's breakfast coffee left over. In the pot on the stove. I keep it on low flame. I like a cup of coffee myself now and then."

"Thank you." I walked over to the long sink with its somewhat stained porcelain and took a package of corn flakes down from the cupboard above it. "Dishes in the cupboard to the right," she said. "Silver in the drawer."

A battered tray of green-painted metal stood propped on the sinkboard. I laid it flat and, aware of her gaze following me, assembled on it a bowl of cereal, topped with milk from the old-fashioned refrigerator, and a cup of black coffee from the pot on the gas stove. "Shall I pour you a cup?"

She shook her head. "You can eat in here if you want. No use in messing up the dining room, is there?"

Was she really afraid I would leave my breakfast things in

the dining room for her to clear away? Or did she want to talk? A glint of curiosity in the little eyes made me suspect the latter. Well, that was all right. I was curious about her, too.

I placed my tray on one end of the table, pulled out a straight chair, and sat down. A sip of the coffee told me it was no worse than most coffee left standing for three hours. "Didn't there used to be a couple named Graham here at the Hall?"

She stripped a pod of its peas and let them fall into the colander. "My Aunt Flora and Uncle John, that was. Great-aunt and uncle, really. They raised me. They live in a cottage at the top of Glen Graham, other side of the village. They're pensioners now."

She laughed. "Mr. Dinswood—he's the trustee for the Hall, lives down in Glasgow—he came up to see Aunt Flora and Uncle John after he heard your mother was coming back here. Wanted them to live in. They told him not for love or money."

Despite my determination to keep cool, I felt my temper rising. I took a spoonful of corn flakes and then said in a neutral tone, "Well, at their age—"

"Oh, they could manage the work all right. Strong as horses, all the Grahams are. But they walked out right after the night it happened. And Aunt Flora says she'd never come back to a house where murder had been done, and where—" She broke off.

Had she been about to say something like, "and where the mistress is just out of the loony bin?" If so, she had thought better of it.

I said coldly, "That happened long ago."

Perhaps she realized she had gone too far, because her tone became friendlier. "Yes, I was only a few months old then. You must have been not much more than a toddler yourself."

I kept my voice level. "I was seven."

For perhaps a minute, while I spooned corn flakes, neither of us spoke. Peas rattled steadily into the colander. Then she asked, "Are you an actress too?"

"No, a schoolteacher."

I could tell that she was pleased that mine was such a prosaic occupation. "In California?"

"No, New York." After a moment I added, "Do you know if my mother is in her room?"

"She drove down to the village to do the marketing. When I came to work here a week ago, I told her right off not to expect me to do the marketing."

A week ago. But Dr. Crandall, the asylum's chief of staff, had told me that my mother had left for Scotland three weeks ago. That meant that for a time my frail mother and her cousin, apparently even frailer, had had to shift for themselves in this house. True, Richard Coventry had been here too, but he didn't look like the sort of man who would lend a willing hand with the housework.

"I told her," Jennie went on, "that the cooking and washing up and keeping the ground floor straight was all I could manage. She'd have to manage the rest herself, unless Mrs. Harnish could help her, and getting downstairs to meals is about all that one can manage. So Mr. Coventry fixed up an old Bentley that's stood there in the garage all these years, and your mother uses it for the marketing."

I thought of how she must hate going to the village. The sudden silence that surely must descend whenever she entered the store. The tight-lipped politeness of the proprietor. The covert stares of the other customers. After this, I'd do the marketing, if she'd let me.

Jennie said, "You'll have to make your own bed, you know."

"Fine. I've been making my own bed all my life."

"Even your mother makes her own bed, and maybe Mr. Coventry's too." She added slyly, "She has the room at the head of the stairs, you know, on your left as you go up, and he has the room next to it."

I ignored that. "Do you know where Mr. Coventry is this morning?"

"Out in the garage, working on his own car." She giggled at some recollection. I wondered if Richard Coventry, now and then, put a friendly arm around Jennie's waist too.

I carried the tray, with its empty bowl and coffee cup, over to the sink. "Just rinse them and put them in the rack," Jennie said. "No point in getting out the dishpan for a few pieces. I'll do them when I wash up after lunch."

"All right." A minute or so later I said, "I'd like to take a long walk today. Would you mind if I put up a lunch for myself?"

She shrugged. "There's bread and cold meat and cheese in the fridge."

She had finished shelling the peas. Despite her reference to multitudinous tasks, she seemed in no hurry to turn to them. She sat there watching me as, at her direction, I found wax paper and a paper bag, and took food from the refrigerator. The two cheese-and-beef sandwiches I made were hefty ones, with plenty of mayonnaise. Breakfast, after all, had been on the slim side.

Suddenly she asked, "Is your mother going to marry Mr. Coventry?"

I said coldly and untruthfully, "I have no idea."

"Oh, come off it. She must have given you some reason for letting him stay here. As Aunt Flora says, you'd think she'd feel that there'd been enough talk about this house."

I lost my temper then. "My mother's plans are her own business. Not my business, or yours, or your Aunt Flora's."

Answering temper flared in her face. She smiled. I have always been a little afraid of people who smile when they are angry. "Oh, he'll marry her, all right, even if she has lost her looks, and is just out of the asylum, and a lot older than him besides. This house and land are worth a lot, you know. And there's plenty of other money too."

Afraid of what I might say or do if I stood there another minute, I tightened my grip on my paper lunch bag, walked out of the kitchen, and pushed open the baize door.

Out on the semicircular portico I halted to let my heartbeats subside. From now on I would try to avoid Jennie as much as possible. If only for my mother's sake, I did not want to risk heightening the girl's natural disagreeableness.

Trying to calm myself, I looked out over the gentle valley. From where I stood I could see the bridge I had crossed the evening before. The stream it spanned issued from a narrow declivity—a glen, I knew the Scots would call it—in the valley's eastern hillside, and then curved to flow south along the valley floor. Apparently there had been heavy rains not too many days ago, because I counted five separate burns rushing down the hillsides across the valley, a rich alebrown except where a rock or some other obstruction broke them into white foam. At the hill's base, although I could not see it from where I stood, I knew that the burns must join a brook, which in turn helped swell the turbulent stream spanning the valley floor. Someday soon I would walk along the valley, but right now it was the moor I wanted to see.

A sudden thought made me turn back into the house. If there had been recent rains, the ground up on the moor might be soggy. I would need something to sit on while I ate my lunch. From the wardrobe in my room I took down my raincoat, a white plastic one. I went down to the broad, neglected-looking lawn and then followed the drive that curved around the corner of the house, passing beside the windows of what I knew was that long-unused drawing room. Up ahead, metal clattered against stone or cement.

A moment later I saw the garage, converted from what once must have been the carriage house. Its wide front door had been raised. My Toyota stood on the cement floor. So did an old but beautifully polished Buick sedan, its hood up. Richard Coventry, in khaki pants and shirt, was bending over the engine. At the sound of my footsteps he straightened and then walked toward me, wiping his grease-stained hands on a piece of old blue cloth he drew from his pocket.

He smiled at me. "Did you get your car keys?" He appeared older here in the sunlight, somewhere in his late forties. And I liked his looks better in work clothes than in those too-studied tweeds. "I left them in the drawer of the hall telephone table."

I shook my head. "I didn't look for them. I'm not going to use my car today. I'm going for a walk on the moor."

"Great day for it."

There were a few seconds of rather strained silence. Then he said, "About last night. I apologize. That's the trouble with show people, even ex-show people. We hype everything, as you Yanks say. When we're gloomy, we're gloomier than other people. When we're jolly, we're jollier. And when we're friendly, we're friendlier, maybe a bit too friendly."

His eyes, rather attractive blue eyes, were meeting mine squarely. He added, "I didn't mean anything by it."

"That's all right." I was beginning to feel that I ought to be the one to apologize—for having had a bad attack of the prudes. And yet last night his face, his smile, his whole manner had seemed quite different—aggressively insinuating, even somehow threatening. Had I, in my fatigue and my shocked disappointment over the alteration in my mother, read things into his words that were not there? Or had he decided that a change of tactics was in order?

I said, to break a silence that again threatened to become awkward, "Is something wrong with your car?"

"Nothing I can't fix. Some trouble with the distributor head." He looked fondly at the Buick. "Isn't she a beauty? A fifty-two. I advertised for days in the London papers before I found her."

I have never understood some people's passion for "classic" cars. Antique cars, yes, with their brasswork and carriage-style lamps and squeeze-bulb horns. But not those cars a few decades old which, for technical reasons that are a closed book to me, are deemed desirable. "Very nice," I said politely, and then added, "You sound like an expert mechanic."

"I used to be a mechanic in a garage in London's East End."

"I thought you used to be an actor."

"That was after I was a mechanic. And I was never much of an actor. That's why I gave it up for the real estate business."

"Is your office in London?"

He nodded. "Our office. I have a partner. I decided to let him run the show for a few weeks." He paused, but when I did not ask why, he went on, "You see, I felt Marcia—I mean, your mother—needed someone to be with her right now. All she's got is that cousin of hers, and she's far more of a burden than a help."

I might have said, "But my mother has me now. There's

no reason why you shouldn't go back to London." I could scarcely say that, though, no matter how much I distrusted him. It was my mother's house, not mine, and if she wanted him to stay here, as she obviously did—

He said, "She's down in the village now, doing the marketing."

"I know. Jennie told me."

He laughed. "So you've met our Jennie. Malicious little baggage, isn't she? But it's a good thing she's here. The first days in this house were awfully hard on Marcia, even with me running the vac and carrying trays."

So he had helped with the housework.

I hesitated, and then asked, "When do you and my mother intend—"

"To get married? I feel we should wait for several weeks, or even months. Marcia needs to feel stronger, more sure of herself." He paused. "I guess the change in her from the way you remembered her must have been a shock to you."

After a moment I said, "Yes."

"It was a shock to me too. She used to be such a lovely little thing. And her voice! It sounded like music when she asked you to pass the salt."

I nodded, remembering how even her speaking voice used to make music in that Beverly Hills house. But there had been no music in my mother's voice last night.

"She looks a hell of a lot better, though, than she did when she was first released from that place. I think that in time she'll come a long way back to what she used to be."

He was wiping grease from his hands again, his gaze directed downward. Had he been in love with her years ago? He sounded like it. Did he love her now? Well, even if he only liked her now, even if he was attracted less to her than to her money, would that be so bad? Certainly not if he made her happy.

I asked abruptly, "Tell me. Do you think my mother was guilty?"

He raised his eyes. They had a suddenly opaque look. After a moment he said, "Of course not. Would I want to marry her if I thought she had killed a man? Believe me, I wouldn't, not even if I thought she'd killed him when she was—off her head."

He shrugged. "It could have been someone coming in from the outside. The terrace door to the study was open. Or it could have been one of the actors, or even actresses, who were here that night. Your father was a fine director, Lisa, but a tough one. He'd have let his own mother's scenes land on the cutting room floor if he thought it would improve a film. He'd told several of his company that he was editing scenes of theirs out of the final version. And an actor scorned can have one hell of a fury."

"Why is it that my mother's lawyer didn't bring that up as a possible motive for—"

"Because Marcia's lawyer didn't know anything about show business. It never occurred to him that an actor might harbor a smoldering, murderous rage just because a few minutes of playing time had been cut from a film."

I said slowly, "Did you ever work in one of my father's films?"

"Sure. I had a bit in his last one, *The Thorn Tree*. A bit so small that if the audience blinked, they'd miss me." He smiled. "But he didn't cut it. Such as it was, it was all there."

Nevertheless, Richard Coventry had had a motive. If he'd been in love with Marcia Deveron, and the husband to whom she was so devoted stood in the way— But no, it was hard to conceive of a man committing murder in hopes of getting a woman, and then standing silently by while she was tried for his crime.

Besides, none of the newspaper or magazine accounts of my mother's case had listed a Richard Coventry among the guests present at Deveron Hall the night of my father's death.

I said, "You weren't invited to that house party here, were you?"

"You mean, because I was only a bit player in the film, and bit players don't get invited to directors' house parties? Ordinarily that's all too true. But Marcia liked me, and invited me, and so I came."

As I looked at him, bewildered, he said, "But I wasn't here that last night. I had an appointment with my dentist in London Monday afternoon, and so I'd left here early Sunday morning."

Obviously he had left. Otherwise he would have been among those questioned by the police. But how far had he gone? Clear to London? After a lapse of eighteen years, it would be almost impossible to prove that he had or had not.

Richard Coventry said, "Give it up, Lisa. You'll do neither yourself nor your mother any good thinking about it. She wants to forget about it. Why don't you forget about it too?"

Perhaps he was right. Although it would gladden my mother's heart, even at this late date, to know she had not killed the man she loved, there was little chance that I or anyone else could give her proof of her innocence.

Perhaps I should give up also my vague idea of abandoning my job in New York to stay here in Scotland. Just by coming all this way, I must have made my mother realize that I loved her and would return to her if she needed me. Unless she really wanted me to stay permanently, when the summer was over I would go back where I belonged.

I said, "Maybe you're right. Maybe I'd better just forget the past."

"I know I'm right."

"Well," I said, turning away, "I think I'll take my walk now."

"Enjoy yourself," Richard Coventry said.

Chapter
Five

Beyond the garage a short, steep path, bordered by heather and bracken and spiny gorse bushes, led up to a tall, gnarled cedar at the hillside's crest. I climbed it, and then stood looking out over the wild landscape I had seen from my bedroom window. A few clouds were drifting across the blue sky. In the altered light, distant patches of heather looked more purple than rosy. And the line of distant mountains was now the color of Concord grapes.

As I struck out across the moor, I realized that I had been wise to bring the raincoat. The ground was not only soggy, little rivulets, only inches wide, trickled through the heather. Already my shoes and the cuffs of my pants were muddy. But that seemed a small matter in this magic landscape.

I found that the moor held miniature delights not visible from my window. Scattered through the heather were small flowers whose names I did not know, pink ones and yellow ones and tiny, bell-shaped blue ones. In an especially boggy spot at the base of a boulder I found a larger flower, tawny-throated and with pale pink petals, which probably was a heath orchid, a moorland flower I had heard of. As for the boulders, they were not really white, but dark gray. It was the flecks of glistening mica on their surfaces which, at a distance and in bright sunlight, gave them that snowy look.

I went on, stepping over the streamlets, pausing now and then to bend above a flower, or to rest my hand against a glistening, sun-warmed boulder, or to scrape accumulated mud from my shoes with a sharp stone. Once I stopped and looked inside a ruined stone hut. The earthen floor was strewn with wisps of straw, and there were great gaps in the thatched roof. From my reading about Scotland I realized that the hut must once have been a "shieling," a summer-time shelter for those tending sheep on the moors. I moved onward, hearing the whisper of wind through the heather, and now and then the tinkle of distant sheep bells, and an odd, whirring sound that I knew must be the thrumming of grouse. And all the time the light kept changing, and the colors of moorland and mountains with it. I began to feel a giddy delight, as if I were sixteen instead of twenty-five.

I had been walking perhaps half an hour when I saw that a few hundred yards to my right the ground seemed to fall away abruptly. A glen, I thought, almost certainly the one from which the turbulent stream emerged to race across the valley floor. As I moved forward, a small black-and-white shape scrambled over the glen's rim and hurtled toward me, barking. I like dogs, and am not afraid of them, but nevertheless I thought it prudent to follow what is rule number one when faced by a strange and on-charging dog. I stood perfectly still.

When he was close enough, the little collie—surely a Border collie?—began to race around me in a circle, barking ferociously but with plumy tail wagging an invitation to friendship. I let him have his fun for a minute or so, and then said, extending my hand, "Cut it out, you faker. Come here."

He gave me a pleased little yelp and trotted toward me, grinning. I scratched him behind his silky ears, and asked the questions that we absurd humans are always asking dogs. What was his name, and where did he come from, and who did he belong to.

From the corner of my eye I saw that perhaps I had the answer to that last question. A man was striding toward me —a tall man whose dark blond hair shone in the sunlight. I straightened up. A moment later I realized that he was Michael MacKelvin, the man who had followed me from the pub the night before.

He halted and called, "Here, Gyp!" Deserting me, the little dog raced back to him and sat down. The man just stood there for a moment, and then started toward me, the collie at his heels. For master as for dog, I waited motionless.

When he reached me, he halted and said, "I hope Gyp didn't frighten you." He was dressed in chinos, and an old gray turtleneck sweater several shades darker than his eyes.

"Only Dobermans frighten me." After a second or two I added, "Am I trespassing on someone's land?"

"As a matter of fact you are on MacKelvin land." He was smiling, and his eyes held none of the faintly hostile alertness I had noticed the night before. Evidently he, like Richard Coventry, had decided upon a change of manner. "But we don't pay much attention to such matters here in Scotland." After a moment he added, "You're Mrs. Marsden's daughter, aren't you?"

"Yes, I'm Lisa Marsden."

"Do you mind telling me why you didn't say so last night?"

I decided to be blunt. "Because I was tired, and anxious, and in no mood for chit-chat. Besides, your warning me about the bridge was only an excuse for trying to find out who I was. You were upset by the thought that I might be Mrs. Marsden's daughter, weren't you?"

A slight flush came into his face. "All right, I was upset. It was on my father's account."

I had already guessed that.

"My father had a slight coronary over a month ago. Maybe it was only coincidence, but it happened the day after he first heard the rumor that your mother was coming back here, and that the trustee was getting Deveron Hall ready for her."

I said coolly, "And why should that distress him so?"

His own voice had become cooler now. "I'm sure you can guess why. The police questioned him about—your father's death. He doesn't like to be reminded of it."

"Why? Was it so traumatic? After all, he wasn't arrested."

"You don't understand. My father has always been a proud man, and a sensitive one. He felt it was a disgrace to the family name that he should be involved in any way in a murder trial."

I wanted to say, "Especially one involving such raffish types as London and Hollywood film people. Is that what you mean?"

Instead I said, "Really? If you MacKelvins are one of the old Highland families, and I am sure you are, then I'm surprised that any of you are so sensitive about such matters. From all I've read, Highland clans used to carve each other up quite regularly."

He looked startled for a moment, and then laughed. "You're right about that. Why, once when the MacKelvins were raiding MacCrae cattle— But that was three hundred years ago. Times change, and Scotsmen with them. Aside from sheep, my father's chief interest is seventeenth-century English poetry. I imagine those tough old Highlanders would have disowned him."

Would they have disowned Michael MacKelvin as well as his father James? I doubted it. Something about his steady gray eyes and his strong-featured face made me feel that, despite his civilized manner and his English public school accent, he had a lot of the toughness of his cattle-raiding ancestors.

I said, "About the police questioning your father. It was because he'd had some long-standing dispute with the Deverons, wasn't it?"

"Yes. It started out as a dispute between my father and David Deveron, your grandfather, almost thirty years ago."

"Over what? Boundaries?"

"No. Sheep."

"You don't mean sheep-stealing!"

"No, of course not. David Deveron had gone out of sheep-raising entirely. He got the idea of using the land instead for growing alfalfa. From all I've heard, it was about the only time your grandfather made a bad investment. He failed to grow a commercial crop—the soil is much too thin—but by the time he gave up he had dumped tons of fertilizer and insecticides on about two hundred acres of land. Some of my father's sheep strayed onto it. More than a hundred of them died, including about a dozen prize ewes. My father demanded compensation. David Deveron refused."

"Well, since the sheep had strayed off their own land—"

"It's as I told you. Boundaries have never meant much up here. Deveron sheep had grazed on MacKelvin land, and vice versa, since back in the last century. My father took David Deveron to court. Deveron hired an expensive Edinburgh lawyer, and won."

I remained silent. I wished those sheep had not been poisoned. I wished that shrewd-eyed man whose portrait I had seen that morning had paid for the sheep. But I didn't want to say so.

"The whole thing became an obsession with my father. After David Deveron died, he tried to collect from the administrator of the estate, and failed again. Two years after that, when he heard that David Deveron's daughter was coming back here with her American husband, he decided to make another attempt. I guess he thought that your father, a foreigner and a newcomer to the Deveron family, might see the matter in a different light. Anyway, he went over to the Hall the first morning after your parents arrived here from London."

"And my father turned him down cold?"

To judge from what Richard Coventry had told me, my father had been a tough, stubborn man. I did not remember him that way. But then, I had been his adored little girl, not a professional associate, or a perhaps-arrogant Scottish aristocrat with a grievance.

"Yes, your father turned him down. I imagine it was a quite stormy interview. I remember—I was fourteen then— how white and shaken my father looked when he came back to Lochnail."

"Lochnail?"

"That's the name of our house, and of the loch beside it, too. When your father was—killed a few nights later, the police felt he might have had a motive, and so they came to interview him."

Silence settled down. Again I was conscious of the faint keening of the wind through the heather, and the thrumming of grouse somewhere not far away. I said, "And when you saw me and guessed who I was, you thought that I might turn out to be another Hatfield to your McCoy."

He looked puzzled. "A Hatfield to— I'm afraid I don't follow."

"The Hatfields and McCoys were two Kentucky mountain families, both of Scottish descent, by the way. They carried on a feud for generations, popping each other off like so many flies."

He smiled. "No, I hadn't expected anything like that." His face sobered. "But I was a little alarmed. You see, the feeling in the village now is that your mother has come back here to—keep herself to herself, as people up here say. But I thought that you might—"

"Make waves? Stir things up?"

"Yes. After all, you were a young child, thousands of miles away, when your father died. I thought you might start asking questions, might try to find out more about what happened that night."

"You mean, what *really* happened, don't you?"

His face stiffened. "Then you don't think the jury reached the right verdict."

"No. I think someone else was guilty. But perhaps almost any daughter would feel that way. Maybe I'm wrong about it. And anyway, I'm not going to try to find out."

That was a resolution which had grown stronger in me as I wandered across the moor. For my own sake as well as my mother's, I would just accept all that had happened to her.

"You're wise," he said quietly. "It's seldom any good comes from raking over the past, and often much harm comes from it." He paused. "Then you don't plan to stay here?"

"Only for the summer. Then I'll go back to New York." Unless, of course, something happened to make me feel I should stay.

After a moment he said, "My father is down in the glen trout fishing. Would you like to meet him?"

Why did he want me to meet him? In the hope that his father would conclude that there was no reason for him to feel disturbed by my presence here? I said, "I would like very much to meet him."

With the little collie trotting beside us, we set off across the soggy ground. He said, "Are you a career girl?" He added quickly, "But I should not have asked it that way. That's considered a sexist phrase, isn't it?"

So the language of women's lib had spread even to the Highlands. I smiled, "It is. But I'll answer your question anyway. Yes, I work. I teach the fourth grade in a public school in Brooklyn. I mean, our kind of public school."

He said, "Then from all I hear about big-city schools in America, you must be brave as well as beautiful."

I said, "You slipped that in quite smoothly." Nevertheless, his compliment pleased me. "But things aren't that bad, at least not in that particular school. Now I won't ask you if you're a career boy. I'll just ask what you do."

He laughed. "Help my father raise sheep. I have a law degree, and intend to practice someday, but right now I am needed here."

We had reached the glen's edge. "Better let me take the coat," he said. With my raincoat over one arm, he guided me with his other hand down a rocky path into fern-smelling dimness and the roar of the swift stream. Gyp pranced ahead of us as we turned right along the stream's edge.

Only a few yards ahead a tall man in old tweeds and a canvas hat, trout rod in hand, stood on a narrow footbridge. I saw him stiffen, and knew that he, like his son, had guessed who I was. He began to reel in his line. As Michael and I stepped onto the bridge, he placed the rod beside a shotgun that leaned against the bridge railing, and then turned toward us.

Immediately I saw that he and Michael strongly resembled each other. But the older man's face was more ascetic—thinner and with more prominent cheekbones and the rather strained-looking eyes of one much given to books. At the moment those eyes, almost the same shade of gray as his son's, held apprehension.

Michael said, "I've brought a pretty girl to meet you, Father. Since she's here just on holiday, I felt I should bring her right now. Miss Marsden, this is my father."

Just on holiday. With that phrase and his cheerful tone, he had conveyed a message: I was no one to worry about. The older man's face relaxed slightly.

But why should James MacKelvin, cleared by the police long ago of any involvement in my father's death, have needed such reassurance? Let it be, I thought; let it be.

Smiling now, he took the hand I offered. "Splendid. I like pretty girls. And you, Miss Marsden, how do you like Scotland?"

"It's hard for me to imagine anyone not liking it." I looked down the narrow glen. The steep, fern-covered hillsides. A gray-trunked rowan tree at the stream's edge. And the stream itself, a limpid brown except where it foamed around boulders. Then I looked at the wicker creel at his feet. "Any luck, Mr. MacKelvin?"

"Fair. I've caught three."

I looked at the shotgun and then said, smiling, "I see you're a hunter too. What sort of game is in season now?"

"Buzzards. It is always open season on those lamb-stealers."

Was it? My impression had been that throughout Britain

birds of prey were on the protected list. Could it be that this scholarly aristocrat felt free to break the law where his beloved sheep were concerned?

He said, "You are on holiday from what, Miss Marsden?"

"Teaching school."

"Splendid!" he said again. "I have always been much interested in education. I am on the board of the local council school. And I am a trustee of St. Philips, the school both my son and I attended. What subject do you teach?"

"Just about all the subjects suitable for ten-year-olds. I teach in what you would call a council school." Seeing his expression, I laughed. "Did you think my field might be English literature, with special emphasis on seventeenth-century poetry?"

He shot Michael a humorous glance. "So my son has told you of my fondness for Donne and Herbert. Do you like them too, Miss Marsden?"

"I'm afraid they are a bit too intellectual for my taste. But I like the Lake Poets, and the Romantics. In fact—" I broke off, embarrassed.

"Yes, Miss Marsden?"

"Well, as I was walking over the moor, I remembered a couple of lines from a poem about Scotland. I probably don't have them right, but they go something like this:

"'Oh for the crags that are wild and majestic,
    The steep, frowning glories of dark Loch na Garr.'"

James MacKelvin said, "You have the lines exactly right, Miss Marsden. Lord Byron, who was Scottish on his mother's side. Byron is not a favorite of mine, but no Scotsman could resist those particular lines." He picked up the creel and slid its strap over his shoulder. "You must come to see us at Lochnail, Miss Marsden. Michael, you must bring her there very soon."

Michael smiled at me. "With the greatest of pleasure."

Did he mean it? Or had I, as far as he was concerned, served my purpose, now that his father was reassured?

"We had best go home now, Michael. There are the accounts to go over."

"I know," his son said. He handed me my raincoat. "Do you think you can get back up the path all right?"

"Yes. It's going down that's tough."

I shook hands with both men and turned away. When I reached the foot of the path to the moor's edge, I looked back. Michael was halfway up the glen's opposite wall, with one hand reached back to clasp the older man's hand and help him up the steep ascent.

Chapter
Six

I spent several more wonderful hours on the moor. Seated on the outspread raincoat, I ate the thick sandwiches, finding them more delicious than the food at the top New York restaurants where my more affluent dates sometimes took me. After that, with the empty paper bag stuffed in my raincoat pocket, I walked for a while. Then, near the ruined stone hut, I spread the coat out again and lay on my back, hands clasped beneath my head, and watched the clouds drift and the distant mountains change from blue to purple and then back to blue. Soaking up the sun, I began to feel a sense of timelessness. There was no troubled past, no uncertain future, only a serene now.

At last I looked at my watch. Since in this northern latitude the sun was still high above the western horizon, I was startled to find that it was almost six o'clock. Quickly I rose, picked up the raincoat, and started toward the distant, gnarled cedar.

When I had descended the path, I saw that the garage door was up. A third car now stood on the cement, an aged Bentley. So my mother had returned. Because I did not want another encounter with Jennie, I decided to go, muddy as I was, to the front entrance. When I reached the portico, I took off my shoes and, carrying them, mounted the steps in my stocking feet.

The glass doors were unlocked. In the dim hall beyond, my mother, still in black pants and sweater, stood beside the heavy mahogany table, telephone pressed to her ear. She gave me that strained little smile. I stood there, waiting for her to finish her conversation. She said, "Yes, Mr. Abernethy, I understand, and I'm sorry I bothered you about it."

The voice at the other end of the line was querulous, and so loud that I could hear every word. "I mailed them to you as soon as I could. It takes time to make lenses like that."

"I understand, Mr. Abernethy. If you'll excuse me now—"

"You ought to get them by the end of the week. When my bill comes, you may think I'm overcharging, but as I say, a job like that—"

"I'm sure it will be all right. Good-bye, Mr. Abernethy." She hung up.

I asked, "Trouble?"

"No, no! I just wondered why Amy's reading glasses hadn't come, so I phoned the optician in London. She broke her others, and she can't read a line without them. It's very hard for her, especially when she's not strong enough to do much besides stay in her room and read."

The bill would be high, the optician had implied. And it would be sent to my mother, not her cousin. I wondered how many of Amy's bills my mother paid.

She said, "Richard told me you went up onto the moor. Did you like it?"

"Loved it." I hesitated, wondering if a mention of James MacKelvin would bring back painful memories. I decided to take the chance. After all, if his son did want to see me again, he would be coming here.

"I met Michael MacKelvin up on the moor. I met his father, too. He was fishing over in the glen."

Her tone was matter-of-fact. "Oh, yes. They're neighbors."

Apparently she had forgotten that James MacKelvin had been questioned concerning his quarrel with my father. She looked at the shoes in my hand, and then down at my pants cuffs. Her strained little smile widened. "You got awfully muddy, didn't you?"

Her words stirred a memory. My small self seated in a room of the Beverly Hills house at a low table strewn with gobs of modeling clay. My beautiful mother, laughter in her voice, standing in the doorway. "Lisa, darling! You look as if you'd fallen in a mud puddle."

"I'll clean them off in the bathroom." I started for the foot of the stairs, and then turned back. "Do we dress for dinner? Long skirts, I mean?"

"I haven't been. But I thought I would tonight, since you're here." She glanced down ruefully at her black pants. "It's time I started paying more attention to my appearance."

She *would* get better. Perhaps my presence here already was helping to make her better. "What time is dinner?"

"Seven-thirty. I wanted to have it later, but Jennie—"

I understood. Jennie wanted to clear away the dinner things and start home while it was still daylight. For all her bold manner, she was unwilling to stay in this house after nightfall. "I'll see you at dinner then," I said, and climbed the stairs.

I had nearly reached my room when the door opposite opened and a woman with short, curly gray hair stepped into the hall. She wore a shapeless, long-sleeved gray cardigan, buttoned to the throat, a brown skirt, and ancient blue carpet slippers. And even in that dim light, she was wearing dark glasses.

I thought of old newspaper photographs I had seen of Amy Deveron. She had been pretty rather than beautiful, with dark eyes and curly dark hair. Despite the lines in her face and the grimness of her expression, I could see traces of those good looks.

I said, "You must be Mrs. Harnish. Or is it all right to call you Cousin Amy?"

She didn't answer that. Instead she said in a low voice, "Why don't you go away?"

After a stunned moment I said, trying to speak pleasantly, "But I just got here."

"You're not doing your mother any good. She didn't want you to come. You'll just make everything harder for her."

I reminded myself that this woman was ill and had a troubled past. "Maybe she didn't want me to come, but I think she's beginning to be glad that I did."

"*He* doesn't want you here."

"Richard Coventry? We had a talk this morning. I don't think he'll mind my staying the rest of the summer."

"You little fool!"

I realized that by little she meant young, not small. Although she was taller than my mother, I was at least two inches taller still.

"You've got your own life to live," she went on in that low voice. "Go back and live it. There's nothing for you here."

Nothing for me here! I thought of the moorland. I thought of my mother slipping into my room last night, and this evening saying that because I was here she would dress for dinner. And I thought of Michael MacKelvin.

"Mrs. Harnish, I'm afraid it's you who doesn't want me here."

"All right! I don't."

"Why?"

"I've told you. Your mother needs to—to rebuild some kind of life. You just make—another emotional burden for her. It's for her sake that I want you to leave."

Was it? More likely it was for her own. She was sick, troubled, and to judge from her clothing, far from rich. Perhaps she was afraid that I might persuade my mother to cut down, or even end, whatever financial support she gave her cousin.

"Go away." There was an almost desperate note in the low voice. "Go back to New York."

"You'll change your mind about me, Mrs. Harnish," I said gently. "Please excuse me now. I must get ready for dinner."

Before I closed the door of my room, I caught a glimpse of her still standing there in the hall.

As I cleaned the mud from my shoes in the bathroom, I told myself that I would just have to try to win Amy over. And if I could not? Well, it wouldn't matter so much. Since she apparently spent most of her time in her room, I seldom would see her. One thing I was sure of. I would say nothing to my mother about my conversation with her cousin.

I set my shoes on the tiled floor to dry and then crossed the bedroom to the wardrobe. No need to wonder which long skirt to wear. I had brought only one with me, a black cotton printed with tiny blue flowers. Worn with my best sweater, a lacy blue Italian knit, it should do nicely.

I laid the skirt on the bed. I opened the drawer of the heavy old bureau, and then let out a strangled scream.

It lay there on its side atop my blue sweater, a dark red furry shape, its one visible eye dull and sightless. A dead squirrel.

For a moment I was aware of nothing except shock and a sick churning in my stomach. Then I thought, "Jennie paying me back for this morning."

No need for this feeling that the dead creature had been meant as a threat. This was just the childish trick of a malicious girl not yet out of her teens.

My first impulse was to dispose of the sweater along with the squirrel. But no, I could not afford to throw away my best sweater. It would wash. Stomach still churning, I reached into the pocket of the raincoat I had thrown across a chair back and took out the paper bag in which I had carried my lunch. I set the bag upright on the floor. From the bureau's empty bottom drawer, I took out the blue lining paper and eased it under the little furry shape.

For the first time I noticed that there was a small wound in the neck. What had made it? A flung, sharp-edged stone? A shotgun pellet? The fang of some other animal? I knew too little of such matters to even attempt a guess. But its death, however met, could not have occurred long ago. The small body was still limp. I funneled the squirrel into the bag and folded over the top. Gingerly I grasped the sweater's lower edge between thumb and forefinger, carried the garment into the bathroom, and dropped it onto the tile. With anger displacing my sense of shock, I opened the big drawer in the wardrobe's base, took out the sneakers I'd placed there the night before, and put them on. Carrying the paper bag, I left my room.

The upper hall was empty. So was the lower one, but as I moved along it, I heard a giggle up ahead, and a scuffling sound.

I stopped in the dining-room doorway. Four plates of gold-banded china had been set, on linen place mats, on the long table. Jennie, struggling playfully in the embrace of a blond youth of about twenty, stood beside the table.

Catching sight of me, they broke apart. Jennie said, "Look who's back!"

I made no response.

"This is Johnny Graham," she said. "He's sort of a distant cousin."

"Distant enough," he said, leering at her.

That sent her into more giggles. Recovering, she said, "This is Miss Marsden, Johnny."

He lifted an imaginary plumed hat from his head and bent low in a sweeping bow. "Your servant, madam."

I nodded coldly.

She pushed at his shoulder, "Johnny, you'll be the death of me yet."

At that moment, I sincerely hoped so.

Her small gray eyes had fastened on the paper bag I held at my side. She asked, smiling, "Didn't you eat your lunch?"

I had no intention of acknowledging what was in the bag. Not for the world would I have given her that satisfaction. "I didn't eat all of it. I was wondering where you put—"

"Table scraps? In the can to the left of the back door. Trash goes into the can at the right. Twice a week Johnny picks up the scraps and takes them to a pig farmer, don't you, Johnny?"

"That's right, luv."

"You weren't supposed to come here until tomorrow."

"Couldn't stay away that long, luv."

I moved on down the hall toward the baize door. I must do something about Jennie. But what? The last thing I could do was burden my mother with the problem.

I thought of the couple who had been in service here eighteen years before. She was their grandniece and ward, Jennie had said. If I approached them in the right way, perhaps they might use whatever influence they had to modify her behavior.

When I stepped outside the back door, I saw that a flatbed truck stood in the graveled space between the house and the garage. Undoubtedly it was Johnny's.

I looked down at the garbage can beside the back step. Somehow I did not want to put the little animal there. I walked around the corner of the garage and climbed the steep path.

The moor had changed again. Now, at past seven in the evening, the lowering sun sent a warm golden light over the heathery earth, the boulders, and the distant blue mountains. I unfolded the paper bag's top. At a boulder's base I placed the bag on its side on the ground, and eased it from beneath the small body. Crumpling up the paper bag for the trash can, I turned and hurried toward the house. I had less than half an hour in which to shower and then dress in the long skirt and the blue nylon blouse which would have to substitute for my Italian sweater.

Chapter
Seven

Gathered around the massive dining-room table, we four presented a motley appearance. My mother wore a long green dress, green eye shadow, and a touch of rouge. Although she still was not the lovely creature of my childhood memories, she did look far more attractive than the strained, white-faced woman who had opened the door of Deveron Hall to me less than twenty-four hours earlier. Amy Harnish, eyes barely visible behind the purple glasses, had exchanged her bedroom slippers for black oxfords, but still wore the drab gray sweater and dark skirt. Richard Coventry, in tan slacks and matching turtleneck and plaid sports jacket, looked ready for a summer cocktail party in the Hamptons.

In the same blue skirt and blouse she had worn all day, Jennie served the meal with more speed than style. I found, though, that she was a good cook. The peas she had shelled that morning were not overdone, and the roast chicken with herb dressing had been cooked to moist perfection.

Nevertheless, since my mother said little and Amy nothing at all, the meal would have been a strained one without Richard Coventry. He asked about my day on the moor, and then used my description of the wildflowers I had seen as a springboard for stories about *A Highland Blossom*, a play in which he long ago toured the small towns of Scotland and northern England. To judge by the lines he quoted, the play had been hilariously bad, and his experiences as its juvenile lead a series of comic disasters—scenery that collapsed upon him, cubbyhole dressing rooms shared with a drunken fellow actor, and a leading lady who, in a fit of rage one night, had thrown a bucket of scrub water over him only a minute or so before he was to walk from the wings onto the stage. The manager, who was also the play's author, had hastily supplied a new line for him to speak when he made his dripping entrance: "Sorry for my appearance, everyone, but I slipped and fell into the brook whilst coming up the lane."

Richard said, "The audience loved it. They kept breaking into howls every few minutes through the rest of the play, even the tragic parts."

Only Amy did not react to his stories. She continued to eat in silence, gaze directed at her plate. But I was laughing out loud, and my mother, as she listened to her fiancé, had a doting smile on her lips.

More and more I could see why she was attracted to him. Again I thought, why not? After all she had been through, perhaps an amusing man, even though he might be a bit of a fortune hunter, was exactly what she needed. As for his being a few years her junior, these days many women, even beautiful and famous ones with a wide range of men from which to choose, did not hesitate to take husbands or lovers many years younger than themselves.

When we were eating our dessert of blackberries and cream, Richard asked, "Are you going to do more exploring tomorrow?"

"Yes. I thought I might drive along the valley, and maybe even drive up a few glens—the ones with roads, I mean."

"A lot of them have roads, but as for what kind of roads—"

The distant sound of the ringing phone made him break off. He pushed back his chair and said, "I'll get it." Apparently answering the phone was another task that Jennie considered not part of her job.

When he returned a few moments later, he smiled at me, one eyebrow lifted. "You haven't wasted any time, have you? A gentleman is asking for you."

Aware of pleasantly accelerated heartbeats, I went down the hall to the phone. As I had hoped, the caller was Michael MacKelvin. "I wondered if you might like to pay a visit to our local pub."

I thought of the silence that had descended upon that cozy pub parlor the night before. Nevertheless, it never occurred to me to refuse his invitation. "That sounds very pleasant."

"Shall I call for you in half an hour? Or is that too soon?"

"Half an hour will be fine." I would have to change. All the women in the pub the night before had been in daytime clothing.

I walked back to the dining room. In the doorway I said, "Will you please excuse me? That was Michael MacKelvin. He wants to take me to the pub."

"Well!" Richard said. "The very top of the local squirearchy, no less."

My mother smiled. "I think that's very nice, dear."

Only her cousin seemed displeased. Despite the masking dark glasses, I could see what seemed to me alarmed protest in her pale face. Obviously she felt that the attentions of an attractive man might ensure my staying here. But I was not going to let Amy's hostility spoil my anticipation of the evening. "All right, then," I said. "I had better get ready."

Half an hour later I opened the door to Michael. Through the lingering daylight we walked down the steps to his car. I saw that it was a dark red Land Rover, a sturdy vehicle well suited to Scotland's rough roads and steep grades. When he had gotten into the driver's seat beside me, he said, "I passed Jennie Graham on the way up from the road."

She must have cleared the table, stacked the dishes for the morning's washing-up, and started home.

"Is it all right with you if we pick her up and take her to the foot of her road?"

"Of course."

We had nearly reached the end of the drive when I saw Jennie trudging ahead of us, a bright red shawl covering her head and hanging down over the back of her blouse and skirt. She looked over her shoulder and then paused at the drive's edge. Michael stopped the car beside her. "Can we give you a lift, Jennie?"

I saw the leap of surprise in her face at sight of me. Then she said, in a tone so meek that it was my turn to be surprised, "Thank you, sir. It's kind of you."

She got into the back seat. As we drove across the bridge and through the little village, she made no attempt to join our conversation about the length of the northern summer day and the fullness of the burns spilling down the hillsides. Less than a mile beyond the village, though, she said, "There's Graham's Glen just ahead, sir. Best not drive up it. It will be getting dark in there now. And the road's bad."

At the junction of the road with an even narrower one that slanted up through the glen, Michael stopped the car. I was aware of a noisy stream, a ghostly white in the gathering dark, rushing down the glen to disappear into a culvert beneath the valley road.

Jennie got out. "Good night, sir. Good night, miss." She looked at me through the fading light, her little eyes no friendlier than before, but touched with a certain respect.

Plainly my being with Michael MacKelvin had increased my status in her eyes. She turned away up the glen.

As we drove back past the village's dozen or so stone or white plaster cottages and its garage and general store, with a public phone booth out front, it occurred to me that he might want to increase my status in the eyes of other members of this little community also. Now that I had assured him that I had no intention of stirring up the past, he wanted to reciprocate by smoothing the way here for me and for my mother. Perhaps that was why he had chosen to take me to the center of Harlaig's social life, the pub.

Whether or not that had been his intention, that was the way it worked out. When we first entered the amber-lighted parlor, all conversation stopped. Almost immediately, though, everyone called out a greeting to Michael, or smiled and nodded, and then resumed their interrupted talk. After a while, as we sat there at our table, the same one he had occupied the night before, individuals and couples drifted over to be introduced and to exchange a few friendly words. I met the greengrocer, the postmistress, several sheep farmers and their wives, and an aged constable who, Michael told me, was Harlaig's entire police force. Each of them asked the same friendly questions—what part of America was I from, how did I like Scotland, had I been to the island of Skye yet, and so on. It was plain that if a MacKelvin was willing to accept Marcia Deveron's daughter, and by extension Marcia Deveron herself, then so were they. I could see that for someone in my anomalous situation, the class consciousness still prevalent in the British Isles might bestow certain advantages.

As for the conversation between the two of us, it centered mainly around New York, a city he had visited ten years before, just after he had left the university. More than once as we talked, the memory of that limp, furry body lying in my bureau drawer flashed through my mind. I did not tell him about it. To do so might spoil the evening, and I was having far too good a time to risk that.

Shortly before eleven o'clock he said, "You made quite an impression on my father."

"Because of Lord Byron?"

"Partly that, I suppose."

"By the way, just where is Loch na Garr with its steep, frowning glories?"

"Damned if I know. Maybe we should go looking for it someday. In the meantime, how would you like to look at Lochnail?"

"The house or the loch?"

"Both."

"Right now?"

"Why not?"

"I'd love it."

The plump woman behind the bar called out, "Time, please, ladies and gentlemen."

Michael looked at my almost-empty glass of Guiness. "Shall we order another before closing?"

"Not for me, thank you."

"Then when you've finished, let's leave."

A few minutes later we stepped out into a flood of moonlight. We drove back though the village, passed the entrance of the glen where Jennie lived, and then turned onto a road that wound up one side of a valley narrower than the one we had left. In its depths I could see the silver ribbon of a stream. In Scotland, apparently, you were never far from the sound or sight of water.

I asked, "Are we on MacKelvin land?"

"We have been ever since we left the main road."

Ahead now I could see a stand of pines, black in the moonlight. Michael told me that his family had not planted the trees. "The government did. It's part of the national reforestation project. Once Scotland was covered with forests. But for centuries the Lowlanders and the English felled timber for ships, and then what few trees were left were cleared away to make sheep pasturage."

For several minutes we drove through the stand of pines. The moon whitened the road ahead of us and struck patches of silvery radiance from the needle-strewn paths stretching away on either side between the orderly rows of trees. Then, abruptly, we emerged onto a graveled drive leading across a broad lawn to a house.

Michael stopped the car. "Perhaps you'd like to look for a moment. Lochnail looks well from here."

I nodded, gaze fixed on the house. The broad horizontal sweep of its two-story façade, set with long rows of mullioned windows that gave back the moonlight, was of some light-colored stone, perhaps gray. Under the full moon, though, it looked blue-white. At each end of the house rose graceful towers with pointed roofs.

I turned to him. "How old is it?"

His smile told me that my awe both pleased and amused him. "Not very; less than two hundred and fifty years. A French architect designed it. Hence those chateaulike round towers, which make it look much older than it is."

After a moment he added, "It was built by another Michael MacKelvin. He'd made the right gamble during the 'Forty-five Rising, and so he became rich enough to replace the old fortified house which once stood here with this one."

"You mean that he sided with George the Second instead of Bonnie Prince Charlie."

"So you know about all that."

"I'm a schoolmarm, remember. We have to know a few things."

We moved up the looping drive to the entrance, got out, and climbed the steps to the flagstone terrace. We had nearly reached the door when it opened. A stooped figure in black trousers and an alpaca jacket stood silhouetted against the warm light behind him. Michael said, as we moved past the old man into the broad hall, "Hugh, I told you you didn't need to wait up."

"I didn't mind, sir. I've been watching the telly ever since Mr. James went to bed."

"I see. This is Miss Marsden, Hugh."

The slightest flicker in the manservant's eyes told me that he knew I was Craig Marsden and Marcia Deveron's daughter. "Good evening, miss." Then, to Michael: "Would you and the young lady be wanting anything?"

Michael looked at me. "A little brandy?"

"That would be nice."

"Please bring it out to the side terrace, Hugh."

"Very well, sir."

Michael and I moved down the hall between rows of portraits, large and small, in gold frames. I asked, "MacKelvins?"

He nodded. "And their wives and husbands."

I glanced at portraits as we passed them. There was one of a much-younger James MacKelvin in Highland kilts, and beside it the portrait of a serene-faced woman dressed in the style of the nineteen-thirties. After that there were men and women in mid-nineteenth-century frock coats and crinolines, Napoleonic-era tight trousers and Empire dresses, Cavalier plumed hats and deep décolletages, and Tudor short, puffed breeches and tiny-waisted farthingales. Several times I saw, looking out over an Elizabethan ruff or from beneath a plumed bonnet, faces that might almost have been that of the man who walked beside me, and other faces, softer ones, that might have been that of the man who fished from the footbridge that afternoon.

I said, "Haven't you had your portrait painted?"

"Not yet. I doubt that I ever will. It seems rather silly, in today's world."

"Besides, your face is well represented here."

"So you noticed that. It's a bit uncanny, knowing that three hundred years ago there was a man who looked enough like you to be your brother."

"That portrait next to your father's, was that your mother?"

"Yes. She died when I was ten. We turn here."

We went down a shorter hall, illuminated only by the light from the broad corridor we had left. He opened double doors—modern ones, of glass—and I stepped past him onto another wide terrace. He said, touching my arm, "Over here."

We moved to the stone balustrade. Below us, at the foot of a gentle slope, lay the loch, a sheet of silver in the moonlight. "Lochnail," he said.

"Is it deep?"

"Very. No one knows how deep. No monster, though. When I was a small boy, I kept hoping one would surface."

Footsteps behind us. I turned to see the manservant carrying a tray laden with two brandy snifters. "You can leave it there, Hugh."

When the old man had set the tray on a round, white-painted metal table a few feet from us, Michael added, "And now please go to bed or back to your telly program. We'll let ourselves out."

"Very well, sir. Good night, Miss Marsden. Good night, Mr. Michael."

Michael handed me one of the glasses. Sipping the fiery liquid, I looked down at the loch. It was so still that when a fish leaped, breaking the silver surface into ripples, I gave a slight start.

Now that I had walked down that portrait-hung corridor, now that I stood here on this moon-flooded terrace, I had a better understanding of Michael's father. A sensitive man like James MacKelvin, conscious of his heritage and of his place and responsibility in the community, might well suffer over being even briefly a suspect in a crime, especially one involving a Hollywood actress and her director husband.

Intending to make some comment upon the beauty of the loch, I turned toward Michael, saw that he was looking down at me, and forgot what I was about to say. "I think I'd better take you home," he said after a moment. "Otherwise I might make a gesture which could be considered corny, under the circumstances. Or do you Yankees still say corny?"

"Sometimes we do."

I knew what he had meant. A full moon, and a man and a woman on a terrace overlooking a lake. It was like a scene from an old Lana Turner movie in which, while music on the sound track swelled to a swooning crescendo, the man swept her into his arms.

I wouldn't have given a damn how corny it was. I wanted to be swept. But what I said was, "Perhaps I had better get home."

We left our glasses on the tray, walked back through that double line of portraits, and out into the moon-flooded night. On the way to my mother's house we said little of importance. But by the time he had opened the door for me, evidently he had decided that the setting was no longer corny, because he kissed me, briefly but soundly.

"When I get home," he said, "I'm going to try to look up Loch na Garr. If it's within a hundred miles, we'll drive to it day after tomorrow. Okay?"

I said, with no idea that that particular excursion would never come to pass, "Very much okay."

I went into the silent house and climbed, although it felt more like floating, up the stairs to my room.

Chapter
Eight

For a moment after I awoke the next morning, I wondered what I was so happy to wake up *to*. Then I remembered. I glanced at my watch, saw it was not yet seven o'clock, and crossed to the east window to look out over the moor. It was another glorious day, completely cloudless at the moment, with the distant mountains standing dark blue on the horizon. Quickly I dressed and went down to the dining room.

This morning I would not have to breakfast on corn flakes. Two covered silver serving dishes, which I hoped contained sausages and scrambled eggs, stood over spirit lamps on the sideboard. There was also a pitcher of orange juice, a rack of toast, and an electric percolator.

There was also Jennie. She knelt beside what was probably a liquor cabinet, languidly dusting its double doors. I said, as pleasantly as I could, "Good morning."

"You're up early, considering."

Considering that I had been out with Michael. Apparently her meekness of the evening before had been a temporary phenomenon, induced solely by Michael's presence. The freckled face she turned to me was as slyly malicious as ever.

I said, "It's far too beautiful a day for lying in bed." I lifted the covers of the serving dishes, saw that they indeed contained eggs and sausage, and helped myself liberally. Then I carried my plate and a glass of orange juice over to one of the table settings on woven straw mats and sat down. "Are the others still upstairs?"

She was sitting back on her heels, dusting forgotten. "Mrs. Marsden and Mrs. Harnish haven't been down. Mr. Coventry had breakfast half an hour ago and then drove off someplace." She went on, without change of tone, "Mr. Michael's the same as engaged, you know—to Lady Antonia Claremont, down in London."

Suddenly the eggs and sausage did not look quite so appetizing. Nevertheless, I ate in silence for several moments before I said, "That's interesting. How do you know?"

"My friend Mary MacHale, she works for a lady the other side of Halaig who takes *The Tattler* and all those magazines. Mary says she saw pictures of Mr. Michael and Lady Antonia dancing at some party Princess Margaret gave at Kensington Palace last spring. And there were pictures of them at a tennis match too, and horseback riding in some park."

Feeling better, I reflected that such photographs were scarcely proof of an engagement. I did not want to argue the point with her, though. I said, "Really?" in a vague tone, and went on eating.

"Of course," Jennie said, "young gentlemen like Mr. Michael want their bit of fun before they get married."

That I could not let pass. I said, fighting to keep my voice calm, "What do you mean?"

She smiled. "Somebody who'd been at the pub saw you and Mr. Michael turn off toward Lochnail last night."

Anger had set my heart to pounding. I said, as casually as I could, "Yes, he wanted to show me his house, and the loch too."

But I hadn't fooled her. She knew she had angered me. I could see the pleasurable knowledge in her face. I said, "Is it all right if I have more sausages?"

"Take all you want." Now that she had scored, she was generous. "Mr. Coventry's had his, and your mother and Mrs. Harnish never touch them." She got to her feet. "Well, I have things to do in the kitchen."

When she had left the room, I did not help myself to more sausages. Instead I poured a cup of coffee and then sat there sipping it and wondering what to do about Jennie. Something obviously had to be done. Self-respect would not allow me to take outright insults. But I could not, in the old phrase, put her in her place lest she walk out of it, leaving my frail mother servantless in this big house. I could not even speak to my mother about it, lest she become upset.

Again I thought of the pair who had been employed here until that summer eighteen years before. Perhaps they had influence with their young grandniece, and would use it. I could make up some excuse for calling on them. Once there, I would not make heavy weather of it. I would just say casually that their niece did not seem to like me, and that I wondered why. Surely it could do no harm, and it might help, at least to the extent that I would no longer discover dead squirrels in my bureau, or find myself accused of supplying altar-bound "young gentlemen" with a "bit of fun."

As I left the dining room and walked back along the hall, I saw a diminutive figure in a pink skirt and sweater coming toward me. The color would have looked well on a brunette or a blond. It clashed with my mother's green eyes and dyed, red-gold hair.

She said, "Good morning, dear. Had your breakfast?"

"Yes. I was wondering. Is there any marketing to do? I could drive down later and do it for you."

She said after a moment, "That would be kind of you, dear. I don't find it quite pleasant—" She paused, and then added, "I'll ask Jennie what she needs, and make out a list. When you're ready to leave, stop by my room. It's at the head of the stairs, on the left as you go up."

I nodded. I had almost said, "I know."

"Did you get your car keys from the hall table?"

"I'll take them up with me."

She smiled and walked on toward the dining room. I moved on to the hall table and opened its drawer. It held not only my car keys, but several old-fashioned skeleton keys. Doubtless they fitted the doors of the various rooms. I picked up my car keys and climbed the stairs.

When I reached my room, I made my bed and laundered not only my lacy-knit sweater but a bra and some panty hose, and hung them over the shower curtain rod. Then I took my sewing kit from the top bureau drawer and mended a broken slip strap and the loose hem of a skirt. It was almost eleven when I knocked on the door of my mother's room.

She opened the door and smiled at me. "Come in, dear." As I stepped past her, she said, "I made out a list, and put it somewhere."

While she rummaged through the papers on a mahogany writing desk, I looked around the room. It was large and comfortable-looking, but surprisingly masculine, with dark brown velvet draperies and a matching spread on the big mahogany bed. Red leather armchairs were drawn up beside a small fireplace of black marble. In one wall there was a second door, no doubt connecting to the next room.

"Oh, here it is. I put it under the telephone. There are only a few things on it. Just have them put on my account."

I took the slip of paper. "This is a nice room."

"Yes. It—it was your grandfather's."

Perhaps she had not wanted to occupy the room that had been hers when she was a young girl in this house, or whatever room it was she shared with my father that long-ago summer. Or perhaps she had chosen this room because— I looked at that connecting door which, thanks to dear Jennie, I knew must lead to Richard Coventry's room. But then, I had decided not to mind about that.

I looked at the list. Flour, baking soda, matches, black pepper, and vinegar. "Does Jennie need any of these things right away? If she doesn't, I may explore for a while before I come back."

"There's no hurry at all. Stay out as long as you like."

When I entered the village store a few minutes later, I was aware of the covert curiosity of a woman customer who stood, filled paper bag in her arms, at the grocery counter, and of another woman who was looking over a rack of magazines. But I felt it was not a hostile curiosity. From behind her grille-fronted cubbyhole, the postmistress I had met at the pub the night before wished me a good morning. And the plump, bald shopkeeper smiled and said, "What can I do for you, Miss Marsden?"

I handed him the list. As he placed each item in a paper bag, he recorded it on a bill pad and then ripped off the carbon copy and deposited it atop the groceries. As I moved toward the door, the postmistress called out, "There's a parcel for your mother, Miss Marsden."

"Thank you. I'll take it to her."

The small box of heavy-duty cardboard she handed me was about four inches long and two inches wide. I dropped it into the pocket of my jacket and then went outside. When I had placed the bag of groceries on the floor of the Toyota, I took out the small box and looked at the return address.

Charles Abernethy, Optician, Regent Street, London. Amy Harnish's reading glasses, undoubtedly. To judge by the package's small size, they were half-lensed granny glasses. I remembered the optician's querulous voice on the phone, telling my mother she could expect the glasses by the end of the week. Evidently Her Majesty's Postal Service had been swifter than he expected.

I sat there behind the wheel, hesitating. I had intended, once the grocery shopping was done, to call on Jennie's great-uncle and aunt. But apparently Amy Harnish was badly in need of her glasses. She might feel a little less resentful of my presence if I took them to her immediately.

I backed the Toyota onto the narrow dirt road and turned toward Deveron Hall. When I reached it, I left my car in front of the steps and walked back along the hall to the kitchen. Jennie, peeling apples at the sink, turned to watch me place the bag on the kitchen table.

"Here are the groceries."

"Thanks. Are you wanting lunch?"

"Not particularly. I had a big breakfast."

She looked disappointed. "I was going to tell you it won't be for nearly three hours yet. Mr. Coventry came back, and he and your mother drove off someplace. They won't be back until two-thirty."

I nodded and left the kitchen.

Upstairs, I tapped on the door opposite my own. Amy Harnish called, "Who is it?"

"Lisa."

About a minute passed before she opened the door. She stood there in the same dark skirt and gray cardigan. In the dim light of the hall, the eyes behind the purplish glasses were completely invisible. "Yes?"

"The postmistress gave me this package. It's addressed to my mother, but I think it's for you."

To my dismay, her mouth shook. Did she resent me so much that she hated my doing a small favor for her? "Thanks," she said, and took the package. "Excuse me now. I've got a headache."

She closed the door in my face.

Chapter
Nine

Half an hour later I saw why the road leading upward through the gloom of Graham's Glen would be dangerous after dark. It was rough, tortuous, and so narrow that I was glad I had the Toyota. In a car with a wider wheelbase, I would have found myself driving with left-hand fenders almost overhanging the road's edge. And the drop on that side, to the small but noisy stream in the glen's depths, was very steep and strewn with boulders and jagged pine stumps.

Often with the car in low gear, I followed the winding, ever climbing road for perhaps ten minutes. Then, turning the last curve, I saw that the road ended before a little house, whitewashed and with a thatched roof, on a level space at the head of the glen. Smoke rose from the stone chimney. On the bare earth in front of the house stood a pickup truck. I recognized it as the one belonging to Jennie's "sort of a distant cousin," Johnny Graham. From somewhere behind the house came the sound of an ax splitting wood.

As I got out of the car, I saw a curtain flutter behind one of the small windows. I moved past the truck, and then stopped short. On one side of the door stood a sort of rack made up of two upright forked sticks supporting a cross pole. From the pole a half-dozen dead squirrels were suspended by their tails.

The sight made me want to turn back to the car. Then I told myself that there need be no connection with yesterday's episode. These squirrels probably had been shot for food. I climbed one step to the scrap of a porch, and knocked on the door.

After a moment it opened. The woman who stood there was white-haired, with a plump, high-colored face and bright blue eyes. She just looked at me, saying nothing whatever.

I asked, "Mrs. Graham?"

"Aye."

"My name is Lisa Marsden."

"We know who you are." No expression in the round face.

Chilled, I said, "I'm sorry. I'm afraid I'm intruding," and started to turn away.

"Since you're here, you might as well come in."

Although not friendly, she was curious. Very well. At least it gave me entree. "Thank you," I said.

The room I entered was a long rectangle with whitewashed walls and no floor except hard-packed earth. Against the wall opposite the door was a rough wooden bed, with a window above it. Through the pane I could see Johnny Graham, ax poised above his blond head for a moment before he brought it down in a swinging arc.

In the center of the room a rough ladder led up to a trap door. Probably there was additional sleeping space up there under the thatch. Otherwise, obviously, the house consisted of just this one room.

"This is my husband," Mrs. Graham said.

I looked at the old man who sat on a ladder-back chair beside the fireplace, gnarled hands crossed over the hooked end of a cane. Of some dark and knotted wood, it looked as if it had been carved many years ago, perhaps by this old man's grandfather.

"How do you do, Mr. Graham?"

He looked up at me from under fierce, bushy eyebrows and nodded. Then he pointed to the rocking chair on the opposite side of the fireplace. "Sit."

I wondered how he would have looked if I had responded, "Bow-wow." Instead I said, "Thank you," and sat down in the rocker. Above the small fire leaping on the hearth, I saw now, hung an iron cooking pot.

Mrs. Graham had come to stand beside me, arms crossed over her ample bosom. I said, "I've taken your chair. Shall I bring that straight one over from against the wall?"

"I have no need to sit. I'm a healthy woman."

I could think of no reply to that. Still, I had to say something to break the silence. "Did you shoot those squirrels hanging outside?"

"Johnny Graham did. He's kin of ours."

"Yes, Jennie told me he was a cousin. He was down at the Hall yesterday."

Again silence. They must be waiting for me to explain my presence. "I'm new here, you know, and so I was out exploring. I knew Jennie lived in this glen. And so," I finished lamely, "I just drove up here."

When Mrs. Graham finally spoke, her words held no acknowledgment of what I had just said. "We used to be in service at the Hall. We walked out the morning after it happened."

"We would have left anyway," her husband said.

"That's right. Working for your grandfather was one thing. He was a decent man, and no more tight-fisted than most. He left us a bit of money in his will."

It must have been a very little bit, to judge by this one-room house and its obviously homemade furniture.

"And your mother seemed nice enough as a girl. Never pert to us, the way that sly-boots cousin of hers tried to be. But both girls were always play acting and talking about going on the stage and the films."

"Too bonnie, both girls," her husband interjected. "Too much looks aren't good for a lass."

"So your mother finally went to London," Mrs. Graham said, "with that Amy following her, and went on the stage there, and then went to Hollywood. We knew that would ruin her."

I could not let that go unchallenged. "Ruin her? Why?"

"Now don't ruffle your feathers at me. You must be all right, no trollop, anyway, or young Mr. MacKelvin wouldn't have walked out with you, at least not to the pub. But we're godly people, and we don't hold with the stage, or the films either. When she came back here alone for her father's funeral— But I guess you don't remember that."

"I remember it vaguely." I had been five then.

"Well, even when she came back here that first time, I could see the change in her."

Of course my mother had changed from the young girl the Grahams remembered. She had been in her late twenties by that time, and a famous star. But unless my childhood memories were all wrong, she had worn her fame lightly and modestly. How could even this puritanical pair have disapproved of her?

"And the next time she came back, with her husband, and after a few days they filled up the house with that Amy he'd given a part in his film, and all those actors and actresses from London—"

"Running in and out of each other's rooms," the old man said, "and drinking, and maybe taking that LSD."

I knew it was no use to point out that LSD was not readily available in those days.

"And your mother and father," Mrs. Graham said, "quarreling in their room over his carrying on with Amy Deveron. Several times I heard her crying, and him shouting at her."

My heart twisted. I thought of how much my mother, loving my father as she did, must have suffered that summer eighteen years before. Her pain must have been all the greater because he had turned to Amy, the cousin she had grown up with, and whose never-very-bright career she had tried to help.

Why had my father begun an affair with Amy? From those old photographs of hers I knew that she had been attractive as a young woman, but she had not had my mother's beauty, and apparently little of my mother's charm and talent. Well, perhaps my father had not been the aggressor. Perhaps Amy pursued him until he had finally given in. Manlike, he would not have wanted to admit even to my mother that he had been the seduced rather than the seducer.

It was hard to think of that drab woman in the purplish glasses as a man-eater. But perhaps she had been before the years, and ill health, and a broken marriage had reduced her to what she was now.

"What happened to both your father and mother was God's judgment upon them." The old man was glaring at me from under those bristly brows. "He broke the seventh commandment, and she broke the first. It is written in the book. 'The wages of sin is death.'"

A thought held me motionless. Religious fanatics often thought of themselves as God's chosen instruments. Could this old man—younger and stronger eighteen years ago—have gone into my father's study that night— Well, that was possible, but not probable. A "chosen instrument" would be likely to proclaim his act afterward, not conceal it all these years.

"It happened long ago," I said. "My father is dead, and my mother has just emerged from the—the hospital. I'd like for her life here to be as pleasant as possible."

Neither of them said anything. In the silence I became aware that the sound of Johnny Graham's ax had ceased some time ago.

With an effort I said, "And there's something else." I could not leave without trying to accomplish the purpose of my visit. "Jennie doesn't seem to—like me. But since she's there, and I am too—"

"It is not with our blessing that she is there." The old man was glaring at me again.

"That is right," his wife said. "We would have tried harder to stop her, except that work is so scarce. And now she can pay us a little for her bed in the loft. But it is terrible to think of an innocent young girl in that house, not just because of your mother but the two she brought with her—that London fellow, and that Amy who'd been her own husband's light-o'-love! We made her promise not to live in, and to start home the minute she stacked the supper dishes."

"And you," her husband said, "if you're a decent lass, you should not be staying there, even though she is your own mother. 'If thy right eye offend thee, pluck it out'!"

I saw how vain it had been to hope that these two might modify Jennie's behavior. To them their niece—fortunately not cursed with "looks"—was a thoroughly good lass. They appeared to know nothing of the Jennie who scuffled amorously in dining rooms and put dead squirrels in bureau drawers. And if I had been unwise enough to try to tell them, they would have called me a slanderer.

I stood up. "Well, I must leave now. Good-bye, Mrs. Graham, Mr. Graham."

The old man nodded to me, but neither of them said anything as I crossed the room and went out the door. The pickup truck was still there, but I saw no sign of Johnny Graham.

I got in the Toyota, turned, and started down the narrow road, berating myself for being twice a fool. A fool not to realize that I might find myself facing a pair of self-righteous fanatics, true descendants of those ferocious Scottish Dissenters who had helped send Mary Stuart to her ultimate beheading and Charles the First to his speedier one. And I had been a fool not to realize that if I failed with that elderly couple, I would make things worse for myself. If they told Jennie of my visit, which they doubtless would, her behavior would become even more outrageous.

I went on down the winding descent. Even though I drove in low gear, I had to apply the brakes before each curve. The sun had withdrawn from the narrow glen. Glancing to my right and downward, I saw that its depths were already steeped in twilight, with its swift stream a ghostly white.

A sharp curve looming ahead. My foot pressed the brake pedal. I had no brakes. My foot went down to the floor.

The little car gathered speed. With terror stiffening my body, I lifted my foot, tried again. No brakes. I abandoned the brake pedal. Hands gripping the wheel, throat rigid, I concentrated on guiding the car around the curve.

It slewed there, the back wheels skidding so close to the canyon's lip that I expected the car to tip over the edge, rear end first. Frantically fighting the wheel, I managed to straighten the car out.

My hurtling descent had been slowed for a moment, but only a moment. The car was picking up speed again, with another curve ahead. I got around that curve, and the next. I was no longer thankful for the Toyota's smallness. In a heavy car, I would have had a better chance. As it was, even if I managed the curves, an especially rough spot on the road might send the light car flipping to the right, to roll over and over to the glen's rocky depths.

So this is what it is like, I thought with an odd detachment, to face your own death. This is what it is like to know that these are your last moments of awareness—of the hillside flying past, of your heart beating wildly—before you lie, a bleeding and lifeless thing, in a tangle of steel wreckage.

Another curve ahead, with the top of a cedar tree rising above the road's lip. I felt a dizzying surge of hope. Hadn't that been the first curve I turned on my way up to the Grahams'? If so, and if the car would hold the road for a few seconds more—

Rear end slewing, the car rounded the curve. Desperately twisting the wheel, I straightened the Toyota out. Ahead was the canyon's mouth, at the foot of a descent so steep that it would be suicidal to attempt a left turn when I emerged from the glen onto the road.

The Toyota shot across the valley road, jolted over the bracken, hit a hummock, and finally stopped, its engine dead.

All I wanted to do was to sit there until my heart stopped hammering and the sweat of terror on my body dried. But I knew the ground beneath the bracken must be soft. Best to get out of there before the tires sunk too deeply. I started the engine, backed onto the road, and drove a few yards until I reached a turnout. Then I was able to stop, cross my shaking arms on the wheel, and rest my head against them.

Chapter
Ten

I stayed like that for several minutes, aware of no sound except my slowing heartbeats and the "pings" of the cooling engine.

Had the brakes failed purely by accident? Perhaps. The car was old. But the London dealer who had sold it to me had seemed a conscientious man. When he learned I intended to drive in the Highlands, he argued against the car I had first selected. It was all right for city driving, he said, but for mountainous country I needed a car that was completely sound mechanically. Better to take this Toyota. To clinch the argument, he had knocked nine pounds off the Toyota's price, so that it had cost me no more than the other car would have.

So, probably not an accident. Then who had sabotaged my car, and when?

I thought of how the sound of Johnny's ax had ceased. Had he circled around the house to my car? I had been facing away from the front windows while I was in the Graham house. So had Mrs. Graham. My car might have been in her husband's line of vision, but how good was that vision? I had judged him to be at least ten years older than his wife, perhaps around eighty.

In all probability, Johnny had supplied the dead squirrel for Jennie's little prank. But there was a vast difference between a prank, however unpleasant, and a deliberate attempt to send someone plunging to her death.

For the first time, it occurred to me that perhaps it had not been Jennie who had put that squirrel in my bureau. Perhaps it had been someone who was more than just malicious, someone who wanted desperately to rid Deveron Hall of my presence. I had arrived there in an uneasy frame of mind, fully aware that my pitiful mother, for my own sake, might not welcome my coming. Under such circumstances, that grisly trick with the squirrel might have been enough to make me leave quietly. But I had shown no sign of leaving, and so sterner measures had been decided upon.

Would one have to be an experienced mechanic, like Richard Coventry, to sabotage a car's brakes? I knew little of such things, but my feeling was that the task would present no difficulty to anyone who made it his business to find out just where to use a wrench or a file.

As for opportunity, probably the garage stood unlocked, just as Deveron Hall itself did. My car had remained in the garage the night of my arrival and all the next day and night, until around eleven this morning. Almost anyone, whether living at Deveron Hall or not, could have worked on the brakes.

My trembling had ceased, and my heart rate slowed almost to normal. I started the Toyota, drove into the village, and stopped beside the petrol pumps in front of the whitewashed, one-story garage.

A blue-eyed, sandy-haired man of about forty came out of the building. I recognized him as one of the people to whom I had been introduced at the pub the night before. "Good afternoon, Miss Marsden. How many would you be wanting?"

"I don't need gas. I mean, petrol. There's something

wrong with my car." Recollection set my voice to shaking. "I was coming down through the glen back there, and all of a sudden I found I had no brakes."

He looked appalled. "Graham's Glen? Why, it's a wonder— Just drive your car inside, I'll have a look."

I drove into the skylighted garage and got out of the car. He lifted the hood. Aware of a trembling weakness in my legs, I went outside and sat down on a bench against the whitewashed wall.

He joined me a few minutes later. "You're right, Miss Marsden. You have no brakes."

"What happened?"

"Well the connection to the—" He broke off. "How much do you know about cars?"

"Only enough to drive one."

"Then I'd better explain. There is something we call a master cylinder. It holds the hydraulic fluid for your brakes. There is a line—I guess you'd call it a little pipe—leading away from the master cylinder, with this connection, sort of a nut, holding it in place. If the connection slips, the fluid leaks out, and all of a sudden you've got no brakes."

"Can you tell whether it just—happened?" A startled look came into his eyes. Then his face became closed, expressionless. I went on, "Or could someone have—"

"Taken a wrench to it? Not likely, is it, Miss Marsden? And there's no way of telling for sure."

"But if someone had used a wrench, wouldn't the dirt on that connection have been disturbed?"

"I didn't see anything like that. Of course, some of the dirt's rubbed off now, because I tightened the connection to see if the threads were okay."

Was he lying? Perhaps not. But if he had seen some evidence that my car had been tampered with, he might not want to admit it. I was not only an outsider here. I was the daughter of a pair whose violent tragedy had brought turmoil and notoriety to this close-knit little community, and set the police to questioning even its most respected citizen. If Marcia Deveron's daughter was about to bring additional trouble here, this man might not want to find himself accused by his neighbors of encouraging her.

I said, "Can you fix my car?"

"I'm afraid not. I'm not set up for it. You see, it's more than your brakes. Your wheels are out of line, too."

I thought of that hummock I'd hit with a spine-jarring jolt as the car ran across the bracken.

"Better to let me have it towed to Dingwall. A garage there can fix it in a day or two."

"All right."

Sitting there in the warm sunlight, I had a chill sense of aloneness. I could not turn to my poor mother for counsel about this. And certainly I would not turn to Richard Coventry, who'd had the knowledge and the best opportunity to tamper with my car, if indeed it had been tampered with.

But there was Michael. I said, "Do you have a phone?"

He nodded. "It's inside."

I went into the garage and looked up the MacKelvins' number in the slim Ross and Cromarty County phone book dangling beside the wall phone. Michael himself answered on the third ring. I said, "I almost had an accident. I'm not hurt, but—"

"Where are you?" His voice was sharp.

I told him.

"I'll be there in ten minutes."

I walked out to the bench and, aware of the sandy-haired man moving about in the garage, stared across the road and the bracken-covered valley to the burns foaming down the opposite hillside. The beauty of my surroundings no longer bemused me. I had a sense of something monstrous moving beneath the surface of things, much as the monster of Michael's childhood imagination had moved invisible beneath the placid surface of Lochnail. A monstrous something that had brought death to my father and eighteen years of living death to my mother. Something that now, perhaps, had reached out for me. But what enraged mind had given birth to it? That of the fanatical old man at the top of Graham's Glen? The mind of that other old man, that fastidious aristocrat, in the beautiful house on the opposite side of the valley? Or had London been the breeding ground of that monstrous something? With one exception, that ex-Hollywood columnist, every one of the guests at that ill-fated house party had been connected with the London stage or the London film industry.

Suddenly it seemed to me urgent that I go down to London. The first thing I would do, of course, would be to visit that pleasant-voiced Dr. Crandall, in the hope that he could tell me more about my mother's case, and about Amy, too, since she frequently had visited my mother. But after that? Well, I had studied those old newspapers and magazines so assiduously that I could remember the names of each of the house party guests. There had been the two character actors who had played my mother's parents in the film. There had been the hitherto obscure young actor who had been her leading man—and then, after the film's exhibition, had dropped back into obscurity again. There had been a young actress whose role the newspaper accounts had not specified. There had been the London-born ex-columnist who had drunk herself out of a job, and there had been Amy. And up until about thirty hours before my father's death, Richard Coventry had been a weekend guest at Deveron Hall.

In all, there had been five guests besides Amy and Richard. Some of those five might no longer be living in London, or anywhere else, for that matter. But if I could talk to even one of them, I might learn more about what had happened at Deveron Hall that long-ago summer night. And I might gain an idea of why, on this sunny afternoon eighteen years later, someone might have hoped to send me hurtling to my death.

As I sat there, I realized I had still another reason for wanting to go to London. I simply was scared. If possible, I wanted to avoid spending even one more night in that house, knowing as little as I did about its other occupants.

The Land Rover drove onto the gravel. Michael opened the door, and I got in beside him. He asked sharply, "What happened?"

I glanced toward the garage. "I'd rather not tell you here." Without comment, he restarted the engine. As we drove through the village and along the straight valley road beyond, I told him of my visit to the Grahams and my wild ride down through the narrow glen. Now and then he asked a question, but mostly he listened in silence, his jaw set and his hands gripping the wheel so hard that the knuckles were whitened.

At last he drove onto a turnout and stopped the car. He said, "I could speak to Donald Campbell." That, I recalled now, was the name of the garage man. "But if he lied to you, he'll keep on lying."

"I suppose so."

"I may be wrong, but if your car was tampered with, I don't think Johnny Graham did it. He's something of a layabout—you know, a good-for-nothing—but I doubt that he would do a vicious thing like that."

I didn't answer. After a moment he said, "I think you should leave that house."

"I intend to, at least for a few days. I think I'll go down to London."

"To see the doctors at your mother's hospital? I think you should."

After a moment I said in a stunned voice, "Michael! You don't think that *Mother* could have—"

"Lisa, listen to me. I can realize how you feel. She's your mother. But you've got to face the fact that a jury decided, after listening for weeks to evidence, psychiatric evidence—"

"I know what they decided." Yes, I knew. And I had nothing to contradict their verdict except the stubborn conviction that the woman who had given me life had never been capable of killing anyone. "But it's ridiculous," I went on, "to think that my mother would go out to the garage and—"

"I'm not suggesting that she did. She could have had someone else do the actual tampering." He paused. "How much do you know about the man she brought with her? Cunningham, or whatever his name is."

"Coventry, Richard Coventry. Very little, except that he used to be an actor. That's how my mother and her cousin met him. He was in that film my father directed in London."

He said earnestly, "When you talk to the doctors at her hospital, tell them what happened this afternoon. They had her under observation for many years. They should have some idea if she's capable of—" He stopped speaking.

Capable, I thought, of trying to arrange her own daughter's death. The idea was as absurd as it was horrifying, but there was no point in telling him so again. "Yes, I'll see someone on the hospital staff. I may stay down in London for several days."

"Why several days?"

"It may take me that long to get an interview at the hospital. Besides, I may do some shopping. I didn't bring many clothes with me."

Best not to tell him that I would go to London determined to try to find evidence that it was someone else—perhaps even that aristocratic fancier of seventeenth-century poetry—who had gone into my father's study that night with murderous rage in his heart.

He said, "There's an evening train from Inverness. We could have dinner there before you leave for London."

An unwelcome thought crossed my mind. Could it be, in spite of our pleasant hours together the evening before, that he had some reason for wanting me to leave as soon as possible? Perhaps he even hoped that after I had talked to the staff at my mother's hospital, I would decide it was best not to come back here at all.

But no, there was nothing but anxious concern in the gray eyes looking into mine. I said, "Thank you. I'd like to leave as soon as I can."

He glanced at his watch, and then turned the ignition key. "It's past three o'clock. I'd better take you to Deveron Hall right now so that you'll have time to pack. I'll pick you up at five."

When I entered the house about twenty minutes later, I saw that the study door stood open. I stopped in the doorway. My mother and Richard Coventry sat in the armchairs beside the unlighted fireplace with a game of double solitaire spread out on the low table between them.

She said, "Hello, dear. Did you have a nice time?"

"Yes, except that something's wrong with my car. I left it

at the garage in the village and called Michael MacKelvin. He brought me home."

"That's too bad," she said vaguely. Then: "You missed lunch, but I'm sure there was food left over."

Until then, I hadn't realized that I'd had no lunch. "I'm not hungry. Besides, Michael is picking me up at five, and so I have to pack. If it's all right with you, I'm going down to London for a few days."

Richard Coventry raised an eyebrow. "With Michael MacKelvin?"

"No, he's going to put me on the train in Inverness." I looked at my mother. "Is that all right?"

Her face had a worried look. "Why, of course, dear. But why are you going? Is there anything wrong?"

"No, nothing. I just want to shop. Besides, I have a wisdom tooth that's acting up." I turned to Richard Coventry. "Could you recommend a London dentist?"

Perhaps he remembered telling me that it was to keep a Monday afternoon dental appointment that he had left the house party that long-ago Sunday morning. From his bland expression, I could not tell whether or not he did. "Try my dentist. Dr. Eric Langtry, on King's Road. I've been going to him for the past twenty years."

"Thanks. I'll try to get an appointment."

My mother still had that worried look. "Shall I help you pack, dear?"

"Thank you, but it won't take me five minutes."

I climbed the stairs. As I crossed my room toward the wardrobe, I glanced through the north window, and then stopped short. Amy Harnish was out there just at the moor's edge, seated motionless on a rock beside the gnarled cedar tree.

What would I see in her face if I told her about my brakes failing that afternoon?

The impulse was overwhelming. I left the room and went down the stairs. My mother and Richard Coventry looked up from their card game, but I did not pause. "Back in a moment," I called to them, and went out the front door.

When I emerged from the steep little path onto the moor, Amy Harnish abruptly stood up and, from behind the purplish glasses, watched my approach. She wore a different skirt today, a plaid one, but the same shapeless gray cardigan.

I said, "Are the reading glasses okay?"

"Yes." After a moment she added, "Thanks."

"I came up to say good-bye. I'm leaving for London tonight."

She said swiftly, "You mean you're going to fly back to New York?"

"No. I'll be back in a few days."

She said nothing. After a moment I added, "I had an unnerving experience this afternoon. I was driving down a steep road when my brakes failed."

Her white face seemed to freeze. After a moment she said, "Doesn't that make you realize you shouldn't come back here?"

"Because my brakes failed? Why should that make me stay away?" When she didn't answer, I said, "Well, Mrs. Harnish?"

"Because you ought to take it as a kind of—sign."

"I'm not superstitious. I don't believe in signs. Besides, I thought it was for my mother's sake that you wanted me to leave here."

She said after a moment, "It is. But I should think that after today you yourself would want to leave."

"I still don't understand, unless— You don't think that someone might have tampered with my car, do you?"

"I never said that!"

As if afraid she might say more, she turned and started away from me. She had gone only a few steps when her right ankle turned under her, and she fell to her hands and knees.

I hurried to her. As I helped her to rise, I asked, "Are you hurt?"

"No. My right ankle is always doing that."

Her dark glasses had fallen off. For a moment her eyes, brown and opaque-looking, met mine. Then I stooped, picked the glasses up from the heather, and gave them to her. As she raised trembling hands to put her glasses back on, the loose cuffs of her sweater fell back along her thin white arms. For the first time I saw the threadlike scars running across the inner sides of both her wrists.

Amy had been unhappy in her marriage, my mother had said. If those were the scars of self-inflicted wounds, as they undoubtedly were, then her marriage must have been unhappy indeed.

Despite her unrelenting hostility toward me, I felt suddenly ashamed of having come out here to confront her. "Does your ankle hurt? Shall I help you back to the house?"

She shook her head.

"Well, good-bye then," I said, and turned away.

Chapter
Eleven

About twenty-four hours later I sat in an office that was both large and pleasant, with paintings of Lake Country scenes hung on its pale green walls. Over the shoulder of the man behind the highly polished desk, I could look through a window to one of those velvety, centuries-old English lawns. Men and women strolled along graveled paths and sat on benches under giant oaks. I might have been in the manager's office at some expensive resort, except for two things. As I came up the walk, I had seen bars on the upper-floor windows of this sprawling, white brick building. And among the strollers out there in the late afternoon sunlight were at least a half-dozen white-uniformed attendants.

Dr. Crandall said, "I was pleased to get your phone call." He was a big man with gray hair, and friendly, surprisingly young blue eyes behind rimless glasses. "Ever since she left here I have been hoping for some word about your mother. How is she getting along?"

"All right, I think."

Something in my tone made his gaze sharpen. "Does she seem depressed?"

I thought of her smiling at Richard Coventry's stories, and sitting with him at the card-strewn table in the study. "Not particularly. Of course, she's much changed from the way I remember her. Much older, and quieter, and—sort of detached." I broke off and then said, "What I came here to find out is—"

What I had come to find out was whether he thought my mother capable, not only of killing her husband, but of trying to kill her daughter too. But I found I could not say that, at least not so bluntly.

"Yes, Miss Marsden?"

"Just—just how insane was my mother?"

"That is a difficult question to answer. In the first place, insanity is a legal term, not a medical one. To us doctors, human behavior ranges over a scale with almost infinite gradations, from that of the healthily functioning human being to that of the murderous paranoiac or the vegetablelike catatonic. It is the law which decides when a person should be declared legally insane—that is, so far removed from normal mental functioning that he should be confined for society's good, or his own."

"I understand. Perhaps I should put it this way. How far was my mother from—normal mental functioning?"

"She'd had an amnesic interval, lasting from some time before until some time after she was found—"

He hesitated. I said, "It's all right, Dr. Crandall. You mean, after she was found with the paperknife in her hand."

"Yes. Just a physical trauma—a blow to the head, say—can wipe out memories just preceding and following the blow, so can a severe emotional trauma. I talked often enough to your mother to satisfy myself that the amnesia is quite genuine. She has no memory of what took place between herself and her husband that night."

I hesitated, and then asked, "Did you ever try hypnotism?"

"In an attempt to find out what really happened? Never. It would have been far too dangerous. Her amnesia was a shield against an unbearable memory. To force her to relive that memory, either by means of drugs or hypnotism, might have shattered her. She might have retreated from reality and permanently."

"I see." After a moment I asked, "Aside from the memory loss, what was she like when she was here?"

"Depressed, withdrawn, apathetic."

A painful picture flashed through my mind: my mother, huddled on the floor in a corner with her head lowered to her updrawn knees. "You mentioned catatonia. Was my mother—"

"Oh, no. She was never that withdrawn."

"Then you would say that, aside from the amnesia, she was just suffering from depression?"

He nodded.

After a moment I said dryly, "But then, she didn't have very much to be cheerful about, did she?"

He shot me a startled look, and then gave a grim little smile. "That is something I have often thought, Miss Marsden. It is far more cruel to send people like your mother to a mental hospital than to prison. Even though she was never assigned to the maximum-care wards, she must always have been aware that she was surrounded by the violent and the hopelessly deteriorated. Under such circumstances, the human ego can become very weak. Hers was so weak that several years ago, after both our medical board and the legal authorities had decided upon her discharge, she refused to leave."

"Refused!"

"Yes. She went on a hunger strike, and we had to force-feed her for a time. Under such circumstances, discharging her became out of the question."

"But why? Why didn't she want to leave?"

"Partly because, no matter what we told her, she felt she could not cope with the outside world. But also—"

"Yes, Dr. Crandall?"

"She had a terror of doing any further harm to your life. She once said to me, soon after she was transferred from the hospital in Perth, 'As long as I'm here, I'm almost the same as dead to my daughter. And that is good. I can't give her father back to her, but I can give her the chance to forget me, and be as happy as she can.'"

My throat felt so tight it was hard to speak. "How did you finally—"

"About two years ago a new anti-depressant drug began to help. No other drugs had been effective in her case. Then, about ten months ago, her cousin began to visit her regularly. That also helped a great deal."

Only ten months ago. Although perhaps my mother had not said so, I had gained the impression that Amy Harnish had visited her for many years. Instead, it was not until my mother began to improve—

"Dr. Crandall, before Mrs. Harnish started coming here, did my mother write to her?"

"Harnish? Oh, yes. The cousin. No, your mother never wrote to anyone while she was here."

"Could Mrs. Harnish have learned in some other way that my mother had improved, and might soon be discharged?"

"Why, I imagine so. Staff members, of course, are not supposed to gossip outside the hospital about patients, but I suppose some of them do, especially in the case of once-famous patients."

"Dr. Crandall, what did you think of Mrs. Harnish?"

"I really had no impression, one way or the other. She seemed a rather colorless person, not at all outgoing."

I thought of the silent woman in the baggy gray sweater. Not at all outgoing seemed an understatement.

I asked, "Did you ever hear either my mother or Mrs. Harnish mention a Richard Coventry?"

"I don't believe so. Who is he?"

"An estate agent, with an office here in London. He used to be an actor. That's how my mother and her cousin first met him." After a moment I added, "My mother intends to marry him."

"Marry!" Obviously the idea both astonished and worried him. "When?"

"Not right away. Richard Coventry told me that he feels my mother needs time to—to adjust to the outside world before she takes such a step."

"I couldn't agree more. What sort of man is he?"

"Middle forties. Good-looking. Amusing in a brash sort of way."

"Well, perhaps he's just the kind of man she needs after her years in this place." He smiled at me. "Anyway, there's not much anyone can do about it, is there? She's on her own now."

"Yes."

I fell silent, afraid that I was overstaying my welcome, and yet aware that I had not touched upon the most important topic of all. Finally I said, with a rush, "Dr. Crandall, do you think that my mother killed my father?"

His face became expressionless. "The law said that she did."

"But what do you say?"

A silence lengthened. Then he said, "I'm not supposed to answer such a question. But I'm going to. No, I don't think she killed him. I don't think she would be capable of killing anyone. I formed that opinion before she'd been here six months, and my subsequent observation of her only strengthened that opinion."

Until now, when the burden slipped from me, I had not known how heavily I had been weighted all these years by a certain thought—the thought that, in spite of my instinctive belief in her innocence, my mother really had wielded that paperknife.

He went on, "Your mother is almost totally lacking in aggression. Or rather, since aggression is part of every human psyche, hers turns inward, onto herself. The result is that she is too generous, too tenderhearted, too prone to let others exploit her. Here is a small example. For a while after she came here, she was a smoker. But she could not refuse other patients who asked for part of her daily ration of cigarettes." He smiled. "Perhaps it was a good thing. Finding herself without cigarettes by noontime each day, she apparently decided to stop smoking."

Too generous, too tenderhearted. A memory flashed through my mind of my mother wailing to my father that she could not, simply could not, bear to fire Bernice. Bernice was our cook, a not-very-good cook who also stole household ornaments to finance her daily transactions with a bookie. I remembered, too, that one of those old fan magazines had cited her as "star most cooperative with the press"—which probably meant that she had tried to answer even the most stupid or impertinent questions asked her by interviewers. I also thought of her perhaps too-trustful relationship with Richard, who might be after her money, and with Cousin Amy, for whom she apparently supplied not only board and room, but other forms of support.

I said slowly, "But if my mother did not kill him—"

"I know. Then someone else did. When I was notified that your mother was to be transferred here from Perth, I read the transcript of her trial. The door to the terrace beside your father's study stood open that night. I think your mother's lawyer hit upon the truth when he suggested that someone came in from the outside—perhaps some thief who demanded money, and then, when your father was slow in producing it—

"But there is no point in speculating about that. The best thing for you to do is to let the past be the past. And the best way you can help your mother is to persuade her to let it be the past."

I nodded, aware now that I wanted to disregard not only the distant past, but the very recent one. On my way here from my hotel, riding on the top deck of a lumbering red bus, I had thought I might tell Dr. Crandall about the squirrel and my wild descent through the glen. Now I found I did not want to, and not just because this pleasant man might think me overimaginative and oversuspicious. At this distance from the Highlands, I myself was beginning to feel I had displayed both those qualities.

What, after all, had happened? A malicious servant girl—I was sure once again that Jennie had done it—had put a dead squirrel in my bureau drawer. The next day the brakes on an old car, bought only a few days earlier, had failed.

True, the dealer had appeared eager to supply me with a car in the best possible mechanical condition. But that might have been a bit of expert salesmanship designed to get rid of a lemon, the Toyota. Perhaps over here as well as in the States, the buyer had best beware when shopping for a used car.

I said, getting to my feet, "I hope I haven't been keeping you from important matters."

"Not at all." Nevertheless, he too promptly stood up.

"Just in case I think of anything more to tell you, will you give me the name of your hotel?"

I gave it to him. We shook hands. Then I went down a brick walk bordered by plane trees, turned to my right, and waited at a bus stop.

As the bus carried me through the misty sunlight, past rows of white stone Georgian houses, past Hyde Park Corner with its statuary and soaring fountains, I realized how profoundly that interview with Dr. Crandall had changed my feelings. He had not only confirmed my estimate of my mother's character, he had given me an explanation of my father's death which I was glad to accept. How much better it was to believe that it had been some wandering predator who had killed my father, rather than anyone close to him.

I had the sense of a cloud lifting from my spirit. Now I was eager to get back to the Highlands I had fled only the day before. And it was not primarily my mother who drew me, nor the moorland stretching away to those blue mountains. It was Michael.

I thought of him at the Inverness restaurant where we had eaten a hurried dinner before my train left. The concern in his face. The way he had interrupted his dessert to go to the phone and make a London hotel reservation for me, "at a nice little place off Sloane Square." The magazines he had bought at a platform newsstand and thrust through the window of my compartment just before the train pulled out.

I had an almost overwhelming desire to take the first train north. But I had best not do that, not yet. After calling Dr. Crandall early that afternoon, I had made two appointments for the next day, one with that dentist on King's Road, the other with Constance Lang, the youngest of the actresses who had been at that house party my parents gave.

When I telephoned her, apparently she had been hoping for a call about an acting assignment. "Oh!" she said. "Then you're not with BBC? What did you say your name was? Marshall?"

"No, Marsden, Lisa Marsden." After a moment I added, "I'm Craig Marsden and Marcia Deveron's daughter."

"Oh!" she said again, but this time her voice held excitement. It made me think that the house party, and my mother's trial, had been a high point in her life.

"Could I see you, Miss Lang?"

"Of course, only it's Mrs. Woodring now. I'm listed under Constance Lang because I sometimes get calls for parts on the telly. Could you come at ten tomorrow morning? The children will be in school then. Just take the bus for St. John's Wood." She told me where to leave the bus and which direction in which to walk to reach her apartment house.

"Thank you, Mrs. Woodring," I had said, and hung up.

Well, I would keep both appointments, but I hoped that they would prove fruitless. I hoped that the dentist would confirm that Richard Coventry had kept an appointment with him only a few hours before, five hundred miles away, my father had been stabbed to death. I hoped that Constance Woodring would tell me nothing to reawaken distrust of my mother's companions, or of anyone else in that tiny Highland community.

I left the bus at Sloane Square and then walked about a hundred yards to Herwick House, one of a row of nineteenth-century town houses converted to flats and to small hotels. The woman manager, a dignified brunette of middle age, wished me a good afternoon from behind her desk in the circular entrance hall. I answered her greeting, and then rode up in the little grille-fronted elevator to the fifth floor.

I had been in my room only a few minutes when the phone rang. "Lisa?"

"Michael!"

"How are you?"

"I'm fine. How are you? How is everything up there?"

"I don't know. I'm down here."

"In London?"

"Yes, on business. I flew down from Fort William this morning."

When we last saw each other, he had made no mention of a possible London trip. Was he—lovely thought—as impatient for our reunion as I was? Then another thought, not at all lovely, crossed my mind. Perhaps he was impatient to learn what I had found out down here, lest it be something that might mean trouble for the elder MacKelvin.

I felt annoyance with myself. How could I think a thing like that about Michael, when only minutes ago I'd resolved not to think such thoughts about anyone?

"Where are you staying in London?"

"A friend's flat. He travels a lot, and so I often use his place when I'm in town. Will you have dinner with me? There's this new restaurant in an old warehouse, right on the Thames. It's a bit too self-consciously Dickensian, but the food is good."

"It sounds wonderful," I said.

Chapter
Twelve

The cluster of glowing white globes which dangled from the restaurant ceiling were like something out of the gaslight era. So were the waitresses in their ankle-length black dresses, starched white aprons, and frilled mob caps. Whenever the wake of some ship plying the Thames reached the piles on which the old warehouse rested, the whole building trembled slightly.

By tacit agreement, as Michael and I ate excellent roast beef, dutchess potatoes, and green salad, we avoided all mention of what had brought me to London. But when we were having coffee, he said, "I stopped by Donald Campbell's before I left Harlaig."

"Oh, yes. The garage man."

"He himself brought up the subject of your brakes. He said he was a little surprised that the connection to the master cylinder had slipped, because that doesn't happen often. But sometimes it does on an old car. He told me he was almost certain that what happened was an accident. And I believe he was sincere."

I wanted to believe it too. Nevertheless I said, "But when I asked him if the brakes could have been tampered with, this odd look came over his face."

"He told me he was startled when you asked that. It made him uneasy, too. Especially in a very small community, people don't like to become involved in any sort of charge against their neighbors."

That explanation of Don Campbell's behavior had already occurred to me. Still, the garage man could have been wrong about why that connection slipped. Or, in spite of Michael's belief in him, he could have been lying deliberately. But the last thing I wanted to do at that moment was to argue with the gray-eyed man across the table from me. And so I said, "I can understand how he feels."

We were both silent for a moment. Then Michael asked, "You've been to the hospital?"

"Yes, this afternoon."

"And?"

"I talked to Dr. Crandall, the chief of staff. He thinks some outsider, probably a thief, came into the study that night. Anyway, he is sure my mother did not do it. He says that in his opinion she is absolutely incapable of violence."

I had expected to see doubt in Michael's face, or even protest. Instead he said, "And he should know, if anyone does." His hand reached across the table to cover mine. "I'm glad, Lisa. That must have been a wonderful thing for you to hear."

"No one else could know how wonderful."

"You must be eager to get back to her. Why don't we fly up there together tomorrow morning?"

I hated to lie to him. But I feared the look I might see on his face—worry, even anger—if I told him about my appointment with the dentist and with Constance Woodring. Now that he at least was satisfied that my near-accident had been just that, he no doubt hoped that I would probe no farther into an old tragedy that had distressed an entire village, and his own father in particular.

"I can't, Michael. I need to have my hair cut and shaped,

and to buy some clothes, and I can't do those things in Harlaig."

"So you can't. Well, perhaps I can manage to stay here a day or two longer myself. Tell me, have you ever seen Kew Gardens?"

"No. This is only the second time I've been in London. And the first time I didn't see much besides the hotel at the airport."

"The first time? Oh, yes, just before you came up to Deveron Hall. Well, would you like to go to Kew tomorrow? It's the nearest thing to the Forest of Arden that I know."

"Would the afternoon be all right? Around two?"

"Of course." He signaled the waitress. "There's a sort of balcony here. Let's have them bring us some brandy or something out there."

On a narrow railed balcony that once had been the warehouse's catwalk, we sat on a bench, sipped our drinks, and looked at the dimly lighted dockside jungle of masts and giant cranes on the river's opposite bank. Below us barges and freighters moved over the black water, the waves from their passage sending tremors through the old building. Other diners came out to stand laughing and chatting against the rail. And yet I had a delightful sense that Michael and I were as alone as we had been on that terrace above Lochnail.

It must have been around eleven when he turned to me there on the bench and asked, "Shall I take you to your hotel now? Or would you like to go to my borrowed flat for a while?"

The smile with which he said it was grave, undemanding. I looked into his eyes for a long moment. They held not just desire, but tenderness too. A responsive yearning quickened by heartbeats. I heard myself say, "I'd like to go to your flat."

About eight-thirty the next morning I walked up King's Road, past the smart boutiques and little restaurants and cinemas. It had been almost two when Michael and I—hands clasped, not saying much, but smiling at each other frequently—had ridden back to my hotel in a cab. But despite the lack of sleep, I did not feel in the least tired. Instead I felt very alive, and found everything delightful—the misty sunlight, the neatly dressed Londoners hurrying toward their jobs, and even the Queen's Pensioners, aged veterans in black and red uniforms sitting on benches outside the Royal Barracks.

When I entered the offices of Eric Langtry, D.D., I found that besides the middle-aged nurse there was only one other person in the waiting room, a man of about thirty who read the London *Times* with that grimly resigned look common to people waiting to see the dentist. By the time he came out of the inner office, though, looking groggy but relieved, three other patients were shifting in their chairs and leafing through magazines.

The nurse said, "Dr. Langtry will see you now, Miss Marsden."

I went into the inner office. A thin, brown-haired man of about fifty turned away from the glass-fronted sterilizer to face me. Evidently he was one of those jovial dentists, because he said, "Will the new witness take the chair, please?"

"There's nothing wrong with my teeth."

He look startled, and then annoyed. "In that case, why are you here? You're not selling something, are you?"

"No, I just wanted some informa—"

"I have ten appointments today with people who do have something wrong with their teeth. And so—"

"I'll pay for the appointment, and I'll take only a few minutes of your time. I just want a bit of information about a patient of yours."

"I don't give out information about my patients. And so, if you'll excuse me—"

"Please! It isn't anything you wouldn't want to tell me. And Mr. Coventry—Mr. Richard Coventry—knew I intended to come here. It's—it's to settle a bet. You see, he was boasting about what a wonderful memory he had. He said he could remember, for instance, the exact date of a dental appointment he'd kept eighteen years ago. I said that was impossible, and he said—"

"How is Dick Coventry?" The dentist was looking friendlier now.

"Fine. He's in Scotland at the moment. He bet me five pounds that if I came to see you while I was here in London, and if you looked up his file, I'd find out he was right."

I had caught his interest. "What was the date he gave you?"

I told him.

He opened a filing cabinet, took out a large card, and, after a moment, handed it to me. "You lose. There it is, July sixth. I recapped a left upper molar for him. How he remembered, I don't know, but what he told you was right."

No, not exactly right. Coventry told me that his had been an afternoon appointment. But according to the card, he had been here at eight-thirty in the morning on that Monday.

For a moment I continued to look down at the card, hoping that my face showed only chagrin, and not the dismayed disappointment I felt. I had hoped to learn that the man my mother intended to marry could not possibly have had anything to do with my father's death. But if, as soon as possible after leaving this office, he had flown to Inverness and hired a car there, he could have been in the vicinity of Deveron Hall by early evening.

I handed the card back to him. "Thank you," I said. "Now if you'll tell me how much to pay the nurse—"

"It's on the house, as you Yanks say. After all, you have to pay Dick five pounds. Give him my regards when you see him, will you?"

"Of course."

He gave me an appraising look. "Well, I'm glad to see that in one way old Dick is still doing all right for himself."

I didn't pretend not to understand his meaning, and I didn't even consider telling him that Richard Coventry was not my lover, but my future stepfather. I just said, "Thank you," and got out of there as quickly as I could.

Down on traffic-filled King's Road I glanced at my watch and saw that it was already a quarter of ten. Constance Woodring might be annoyed, and therefore less cooperative, if I arrived late. I hailed a cab.

About twenty minutes later the cab left me before a block of flats in that pleasant, tree-shaded section of London known as St. John's Wood. In the foyer I pressed the bell beneath the name plate of a Mr. and Mrs. William Woodring, and then waited until a woman's voice told me over the intercom to walk back along the hall to the rear flat on my right.

I found her standing in her flat's doorway, a slender blonde whom I would have judged to be about thirty, if I hadn't known that she must be almost a decade older. She led me past a child's bicycle leaning against the wall of a tiny foyer, and then into a not-much-larger living room that one might have called cozy. The divan and armchairs were strewn with toss pillows of various shapes and sizes, and several small tables and the mantelpiece above the gasfire held photographs, including several large ones of my hostess.

When she had sat down on the divan and I in an armchair with a pillow in the shape of a large green frog wedged uncomfortably at my back, she smiled at me and said, "So you're Craig and Marcia's daughter. You look a lot like your father."

"Yes, I know."

"I heard Marcia was discharged from the hospital not long ago. How is she getting along?"

"All right, I think. How is it you heard of her being discharged?"

"Somebody at BBC told me; I don't remember who. These things get around."

The look in her blue eyes told me that she was eager to learn the purpose of my visit. I said, "It's about my mother that I've come here. If you can tell me anything I don't know about what happened that—that night, I'd appreciate hearing it."

"Of course. But just exactly what—"

"Maybe I'd better explain that I have never believed she was the one who killed my father."

Something showed briefly in her eyes. Amazement? Pity? Something else? It was gone before I could identify it. She said, "I can understand how you'd feel that way, and not just because she's your mother. Why, the rest of us could scarcely believe it. She'd always been such a nice person, not like most of the other women in this business who make it to the top. Of course, we all knew she was very angry and hurt about Craig and—" She broke off.

I said, "You don't have to stop. You mean, she was angry about my father and Amy Deveron."

"Yes. I think she was especially upset because Amy was her cousin, and somebody she'd tried to help. It wasn't as if she'd been just another of—" Again she didn't finish her sentence.

Another of my father's infidelities? Was that what she had meant? Knowing how my mother had loved him, I hoped not. But after all, he had been an attractive and powerful man, surrounded by beautiful women.

"Anyway," she went on, "Marcia didn't speak or even look at him at dinner that night, and right after dinner Craig said he was going into the study to make some calls to London. The rest of us went into the drawing room, and we rolled back the rugs and danced, sometimes to records and sometimes with me playing the piano."

"As I understand it, all of you didn't stay in the drawing room the whole evening."

"That's right. I think I was the only one who stayed there the whole time." A certain alertness had come into her eyes, as if she thought my words had held a veiled accusation. "The others kept wandering in and out, up to their rooms, and back to the kitchen to get more ice from the fridge. That sour-faced old Scotsman and his wife who were in service there had gone to bed. Anyway, around eleven o'clock Steven Carr went out into the hall, and saw that the study door was partly open."

Steven Carr, the young actor who had been my mother's leading man in *The Thorn Tree*.

"I remember I'd just finished playing 'Smoke Gets in Your Eyes' when I heard Steven shout, 'Oh, my God!' The rest of us rushed out in the hall, and— But I guess I don't need to go on with that."

No, she did not. Sitting here opposite this woman who had actually seen my mother standing, the knife in her hand

and her green eyes dazed, made the scene even more vivid in my imagination.

After a while I said, "And you can't remember anything else? Anything that—that might indicate that someone else killed him?"

Her reply was a bit slow in coming. "No, dear. I'm sorry."

"Maybe some of the others who were there that night could tell me something. Do you know if any of them are in London?"

"Well, Rosemary Miles and Clarence Renfrew can't help you. They played Marcia's parents in the film, and they're both dead. But Steven Carr is here. He's in a play at one of those experimental theaters. The Black Masque, it's called, and it's in what used to be a sporting goods store. It's like off-off-Broadway in New York."

Her smile held a touch of malice. "Poor Steven. I imagine he still thinks he's going to set the theatrical world on fire any day now. And Cluny Cartridge is still in London," she went on. "In fact, she lives here in St. John's Wood in a top-story flat in one of those posh buildings down by the canal."

"The Hollywood gossip columnist? The one who was born in London?"

"Ex-columnist. She was ex even eighteen years ago. After her syndicate managed to break her contract, she came back here. You wouldn't know this, but in her day she was a worse hatchet woman than Hedda Hopper and Louella Parsons put together. Somehow, though, she always said nice things about Craig Marsden and Marcia Deveron in her column. I guess that's why they asked her up to Scotland."

"Could I have her address?"

"Of course." She reached in the drawer of a table at one end of the divan and took out a scrap of paper and a pencil.

"Just walk down to the canal," she said as she wrote, "and turn left."

I thanked her and rose to leave. Out in the foyer, she suddenly put her hand on my arm. "Look. Marcia was always nice to me. And I like you for not believing that she— Anyway, I do know something, and I'm going to tell you even though perhaps I shouldn't."

I waited.

"Cluny Cartridge was flat broke when she came back here from the States. She lived in a bed-sitter on Edgeware Road. But soon after your mother's trial she moved into a smart flat in Belgravia, and then to this one in St. John's Wood. She hasn't worked in years, and she drinks like a fish, and yet she still seems to have plenty of money. Maybe it's just coincidence. Maybe she just happened to inherit money from someone at that particular time. But I thought of it while we were talking, and I wouldn't feel right if I didn't mention it to you."

I think I must have had some premonition about Cluny Cartridge. At least I know that, as I stood there in that little foyer, I almost wished that Constance Woodring had kept that bit of information to herself. I thanked her again, said good-bye, and left the apartment house.

It was still not eleven. If Cluny Cartridge was at home, and would see me, I would be able to talk to her and still get back to my hotel in time for my date with Michael. I walked down the sloping sidewalk to where the boulevard paralleled a broad canal, with a barrel-laden barge and a lone man in a racing scull breaking its smooth surface. Then I turned to my left.

The many-storied white brick building where Cluny Cartridge lived was grand indeed, set well back from the street with a drive curving around a flower-bordered fountain to the glass-walled lobby. In front of the glass wall, a doorman dressed somewhat like a general in pre-Revolutionary Russia stopped his slow pacing to watch my approach.

Miss Cartridge was "on holiday," he told me, but was expected to return the next day.

I turned back toward the street, relieved that I could not see the inexplicably rich Miss Cartridge. For the rest of the day, at least I would not have to think about anything or anyone except Michael.

Chapter
Thirteen

Like the Forest of Arden, Michael had said. And Kew was like that, once we had left behind us the area of broad lawns, flower beds bright with marigolds and scarlet sage, and benches filled with people reading, chatting, or tilting their faces, eyes closed, up to the sunlight. We wandered along shadowy paths between giant oaks and evergreens, and skirted ponds where mallards and wood ducks swam, or preened their feathers on the banks. Finally, despite a sign that warned of falling tree branches, we took an obviously little-used path. At its end we found ourselves beside a small pond, with no living creature in sight except a white duck with a red head—a smew, Michael told me—who swam toward us, plainly hopeful of a handout.

We sat down on the grassy bank. "I came prepared," Michael said, reaching into his jacket pocket. He handed me a small breakfast roll wrapped in a paper napkin. For a while I tossed bits of bread and watched the smew devour them. Then I felt Michael's gaze on my face, turned to look at him, and forgot all about the duck.

Our eyes held for a long, unsmiling moment. Then voices sounded nearby, and we both looked straight ahead. Two middle-aged women, looking very English in their dark skirts and cardigans, one yellow and one blue, emerged from a path on the other side of the pond. Deserting us, the duck swam toward them. They began to toss popcorn into the water.

Michael said, "I had a call from my father this morning. He wants me back there right away. Some sort of trouble with the agent who contracted to buy our sheep. I'm flying up to Inverness tonight."

"I'm sorry."

I was. At the same time, I felt a measure of relief. With Michael gone from London, I would have no trouble in arranging my time so as to see both Steven Carr and Cluny Cartridge.

"Did you get your hair cut?"

"Not yet."

"Why not give it a miss, and fly north with me tonight? Your hair looks lovely just the way it is."

"It won't look lovely a week or so from now."

"Well, have it your way."

For several seconds we both looked at the popcorn-tossing women and the bobbing red head of the voracious smew. Then Michael said abruptly, "About last night."

I felt a cold tightness in the pit of my stomach. Was he going to tell me that he thought we had "made a mistake"?

"What about last night?"

"It was wonderful. But I find that I'm in love with you. I want a more permanent arrangement."

Tension had tightened my throat. I asked, "What sort of arrangement?"

He said, gaze still fixed on the popcorn-gobbling duck, "Well, what is your opinion of marriage?"

Happiness held me silent for several seconds. Then I said, "Favorable, on the whole. But aren't you being teddibly un-British? I thought that over here people gave long and earnest thought to such matters."

"My thought may not have been long, but believe me, it has been earnest. I have this feeling that for one reason or another you may disappear just as suddenly as you appeared. And if you go rushing back to New York— Well, for all I know there is some man there—"

"If you mean men I date, there are several of them, none of them important to me."

He turned his head then and gave me a relieved smile. "Fine. Several are nothing to worry about." After a moment he added, "Well?"

"There's your father. What would he think?"

"He wouldn't like the idea, at least not at first, even though he likes you. He's had someone else in mind."

"Lady Antonia?"

"Now who told you about her?"

"Jennie."

"It would be Jennie. Well, Antonia is a beautiful girl, and a nice one. But as I told my father, there are two things wrong with her. She's one of those compulsive talkers. She talks in a steady stream, until not only your ears but your brain grows numb, and you wouldn't know what to say to her even if she paused long enough to listen. The second thing wrong is that I don't love her."

After a moment he added, "Will you at least keep in mind what I've said?"

Keep it in mind! I'd keep it hugged to my heart. "Yes," I said.

We stayed out of each other's arms until the women, after tidily stowing away the empty popcorn bags in their purses, turned and disappeared along the path.

A little after four, he took me back to my hotel and left me there. In a blissful daze, I went up to my room, sat on the bed's edge, and stared at the telephone. I didn't want to talk to Steven Carr. I didn't want to talk to anyone. But better to do it. Better not to have left any loose ends here when I finally hurried up to Scotland, and to Michael.

There were three Steven Carrs in the London phone book. The first one told me, in an elderly sounding voice, that he had never heard of anyone named Craig Marsden. The second Carr was the right one.

"Steven Carr here," he said in a deep, musical voice that sounded vaguely familiar.

"Hello, Mr. Carr. My name is Lisa Marsden. I'm Craig Marsden's daughter."

"Well, well, well!" Like Constance Woodring, he sounded excited and curious. But his voice also held an unmistakable note of hostility. "Who put you onto me?"

"Constance Woodring told me you were still in London."

"Oh, *her!* Well, what can I do for you, Craig Marsden's daughter?"

"Could I meet you somewhere tomorrow and talk to you for a few minutes?"

"I suppose so. Won't ask you to my digs. They're not suitable for entertaining a lady." I pictured one of those "bed-sitters" Constance Woodring had mentioned. "And I'm all tied up for lunch."

Tied up? Or too broke?

"I know. I have a matinee tomorrow. Why don't you come? We can talk in the dressing room during the interval. There are only two acts, and so the interval is a long one."

"Fine. What is the address of the theater?"

He gave it to me. I hung up, and then looked in the advertising section of the phone book for a hairdresser in the

Sloane Square area. Since I had nothing else to do the next morning, I might as well get that haircut.

I made a ten o'clock appointment. Then I was free to lie back, look unseeingly at the overhead light fixture, and think of what it was going to be like to be Michael MacKelvin's wife.

Chapter
Fourteen

The next afternoon, fresh from the hairdresser's, I traveled thriftily but too slowly by bus up to Marylebone Road. Thus by the time I found the sports-shop-turned-theater on a side street, it was past two-thirty. A crudely constructed box office stood in the little entryway. I gave the equivalent of about eighty-five cents to the box office girl, a brunette in a purple blouse that had not been ironed and with long hair that looked as if it had been, and received in return, not a ticket, but a printed program on a sheet of cheap paper.

I went inside, parted a pair of green plush curtains, and entered a long narrow room. A scattered audience occupied about two dozen of the wooden folding chairs set in rows. On the otherwise bare stage at the far end of the room, two actors sat behind the tables. The older man, dark and stocky and rather handsome, was looking out over the heads of the audience and speaking in the deeply musical voice I had heard over the phone.

I slipped into a chair. After a moment Steven Carr fell silent, and the younger man began to speak, also staring not at but over the audience. Soon I realized that they were supposed to be father and son, talking in scatological but dull detail about the woman they both loved. Since only two names were listed on the playbill, obviously we would never see the woman herself. Perhaps the avante-garde drama is over my head, but I found it hard to understand why the audience was even that large.

At the end of the act, a curtain did not come down. Perhaps there was no curtain. The footlights dimmed, the actors walked off the stage, and the house lights came on. The applause was perfunctory except for two men—friends of the author, perhaps, or the actors—who pounded their palms together and shouted, "Bravo!" I went down to a door at one end of the stage and knocked.

Steven Carr opened the door. "Come in, dear."

I stepped past him into what must have been the shop's storeroom. Stacked wooden crates still stood at its far end. Just inside the entrance, a naked light bulb shone down on two makeup-strewn tables, backed by a long mirror hung on the wall. At one of them the younger actor sat thickening the line of his eyebrows with a dark pencil.

"Ronnie," Steven Carr said, "would you excuse us?"

"Righto." Ronnie laid down the pencil, smiled at me, and went out into the auditorium. Steven Carr waved me to the chair Ronnie had vacated, and moved his own chair out from the other table.

When we sat facing each other, I saw that he was not quite as good-looking as he had appeared from out front. The toupee which hid his receding hairline was obvious, and his mouth was discontented-looking and too thin.

He asked, "What do you think of the play so far?"

I had prepared myself for that question. "I've never seen anything like it. It's so original, having the two characters never speak to or even look at each other."

He nodded. "It was the originality that made me think it might go. But it hasn't," he said gloomily. "We close Saturday."

"Oh, I am sorry." When he didn't answer, I went on, "I wanted to see you, Mr. Carr, because—"

"Steven, dear. Call me Steven. And I know why you're here. After you called me, I called Connie Woodring, and she told me you were trying to find out more about that house party. By the way, what did you think of Connie?"

"Why, she seemed very nice, and so pretty and young-looking."

"Yes, I don't know how she does it." He glanced into the mirror, and then looked back at me. "But she's a scheming little bitch, you know, always hoping the casting-couch route will get her to the top. Why, even with Craig—"

He broke off. I said, steeling myself, "Go on."

"Well, she'd had a little fling with him. Not a big thing, like what he had going with Amy Deveron before he'd finished the film. I gather it was only a one-night stand. And she hadn't gotten her part in the film that way. I doubt that anyone ever slept her way into a Craig Marsden film.

"But Connie did hope," he went on, "to get a Hollywood contract out of it. He wouldn't give it to her. I suppose he felt she was all right for that one part, but nothing more. She was furious. In fact, I've always had a private theory that she was really the one who—"

Again he stopped speaking. I said, "Do you mean the one who killed my father?"

"Yes, I'd bet on little Connie."

I discounted his words. Obviously he both disliked and envied Constance Woodring. I said, "Why Connie, rather than Amy Deveron?"

"Why should Amy have killed him? He seemed serious about her. There were rumors he was going to divorce Marcia so he could marry her. Amy had everything to lose by his death. In fact, she did lose. Never got any other role at all, as far as I know, but just dropped out of sight." He paused. "Do you happen to know what became of her?"

I said after a moment, "She's divorced from a man named Harnish, and living up in Scotland with my mother."

He whistled. "Not only living with, I'll bet, but *off*. Well, Marcia was always like that. Too soft for her own good."

I asked, "What did you think of my father?"

His thin mouth tightened. "Look, luv. I didn't kill him, and there's not one chance in a million that anyone could hang it on me. And so I don't mind telling you that I hated him. He cut my best scenes, the ones that would have put me right at the top overnight."

He turned to look broodingly at himself in the mirror. "If Craig Marsden hadn't ruined the one good chance I ever had, today I might have been another Bur—" He checked himself.

Now I knew who he reminded me of. He looked and sounded like a slightly effeminate Richard Burton.

He had turned back to me. "Connie said you planned to see old Cluny Cartridge."

"If I can."

"Well, I wish you luck. From all I've heard, she never sees anyone these days. Never totters out of her posh digs except to walk her dog after dark. Years ago, though—about six months after your mother's trial—I ran into her on Oxford Street. I was so curious about where she got her money that I took her to a pub and started feeding her drinks. That woman has a hollow leg. She was into me for almost five pounds before she told me that a Canadian oil company she'd invested in while she was still in Hollywood discovered a big new field, and her stock increased twenty times in value. And I didn't believe that."

"What did you believe?"

He shrugged. "I don't know, but not that."

"Do you think she could somehow have gotten a large sum of money out of my father?"

"Yes, luv. Now that you mention it, I do. Those old-style Hollywood columnists were good at extortion. They'd manage to let a star know that if he came through with a nice Christmas present—a sable coat, say—the details of that little fling of his down in Palm Springs or wherever wouldn't appear in print. Maybe she'd gotten a large sum of money out of Craig Marsden that way. Maybe he had second thoughts, and demanded it back, and even threatened to call the police. And maybe then she— Anyway, that's another theory I've played around with, although I still bet on little Connie."

I said slowly, "You were the one who found my mother standing there with the knife in her hand. And yet you don't believe she killed him, do you?"

"Marcia? Heavens to Betsy, no. In or out of her right mind, Marcia wouldn't hurt a fly." He looked at his wrist watch. "And now, luv, I'll have to chase you out of here. The second act goes on in a few minutes."

I rose, and he too got to his feet. "Thank you very much indeed," I said. "I'm sorry I can't stay for the last act. I want to see Cluny Cartridge this afternoon if I can."

He gave me a bleak little smile. "The play stinks, doesn't it?"

"Well, I don't know much about plays—"

"It stinks. But you have to keep trying, keep hoping that something will catch on with critics, or the public, or *some-body*. Well, good-bye. Give my love to your mother."

Chapter
Fifteen

I walked back to Marylebone Road and then stood hesitating beside a telephone call box. Should I phone ahead? No, I decided. Cluny Cartridge would find it harder not to see me if I could tell her I was downstairs in her apartment house.

A long bus ride later, I was again in St. John's Wood. Yes, the Russian general told me, Miss Cartridge had returned that morning. "Go in and speak to Mr. Paisley at the reception desk, miss. He will announce you."

Once I stepped beyond the glass wall, I felt I knew why Cluny Cartridge had chosen this particular apartment house. With thick blue plush carpeting, and indoor fountain, and gilded nude statues holding candelabra aloft among the potted palms, it looked far more like Wilshire Boulevard than London. There was even Muzak, softly paying "The Third Man" theme.

The neat, eyeglassed man behind a glass-topped desk against one wall took my name and then picked up a phone. "Miss Cartridge? A Miss Marsden is here to see you."

After a moment I heard her reply, loud and harsh and yet slurred. "All right, put her on."

With a nod of his head, the man indicated a row of phones on a wall shelf, separated from each other by glass partitions. "Just pick up any phone, Miss Marsden."

Seconds later that slurred voice said in my ear, "If you're from the hospital, you're wasting your time. I said no, and I mean no."

"I'm not from any hospital, Miss Cartridge."

"What did Paisley say your name was?"

"Marsden, Lisa Marsden. Craig Marsden was my father." She was silent for so long that I said, "Miss Cartridge? Are you still there?"

"Yes, I'm still here. I was trying to decide— Hell, there's no reason now why I shouldn't see you. Not one damn reason. Come on up. It's Twelve-A, on the top floor."

I heard a click. Recluse or not, she was too curious not to see me. I walked back to where one of three elevators stood with its door open. Except for the piped-in orchestra, now playing "La Vie en Rose," the uniformed operator and I rode in silence to the top floor.

When I pushed the bell of 12-A, I heard soft chimes, followed immediately by the shrill yapping of a dog. After a few seconds, the door opened. A tall, thin woman, with a lined face and bitter dark eyes framed by improbably black hair, stared at me silently. At last she said, through the dog's high-pitched barks, "You're Craig Marsden's kid all right. Come in."

I stepped past her into a huge room which, except for a few color accents provided by sofa cushions and glazed pottery vases, was all white, like a set from a nineteen-thirties movie. White wall-to-wall carpeting, white upholstered sofas and chairs, white walls hung with landscapes and still lifes in delicate pastels. From the glass front wall, I realized, there must be a fine view of the canal and the park beyond.

In its way, it was a beautiful room. But the moment I stepped into it, I felt so oppressed by something in the atmosphere, some long-standing depression or bitterness or guilt, that I wished I hadn't come here.

The dog was still yapping. A fat Pekingese, he sat on a soiled white cushion on the floor beside an armchair. Evidently it was the chair Cluny Cartridge had just vacated, because on the other side of it, within easy reach, stood a table holding a half-empty bottle of bourbon, a pitcher of water, and two glasses, one empty, the other filled with deep amber liquid.

She said to the dog, "Shut up, Lovey." Then to me: "Have a seat."

I sat down in a Louis Quinze-style chair covered in white satin. Lovey, no longer yapping, but making peevish noises in his throat, kept his bulging eyes fixed upon me. I looked back at him, realizing that at last I'd met a dog I didn't like.

She said, tilting the bourbon bottle over the empty glass, "Drink?"

I had best not refuse, if I wanted her to talk. "Yes, please. A light one."

She poured a little bourbon, filled the rest of the glass with water, and handed it to me. Then she tipped more bourbon into her own drink and sat down. "The doorman said someone asked for me yesterday. Was it you?"

"Yes. He said you were on holiday, but would be back today."

"I wasn't on holiday." She took a long swallow of her drink, tilted her head back, and then looked at me with those bitter dark eyes. "I just told them that. I was in the hospital."

"I'm sorry that you've been ill."

"Have been, and am."

I looked at her glass. "Then is it a good idea—"

"At this point, it doesn't matter a bit." She took another

swallow, and then said, "They want me to have an opera-
tion. I told them to shove it."

Appalled, not knowing what to say, I sat there in silence
and looked at the dog. He had stretched out on the cushion
now, head on his forepaws, and wheezing through his
mashed-in nose.

Cluny Cartridge said, "Is Marcia still in that place?"

"No, she was discharged several weeks ago. She's in Scotland now."

"Not in that same house!"

"Yes."

"God! Talk about returning to the scene of the crime!"

Anger, sudden and unexpected, surged through me. "I
don't think my mother committed any crime. And neither
does the chief of staff at that hospital."

"Did I say it was her crime? In fact, I'm damn sure it
wasn't."

I leaned forward. "What do you mean, damn sure?"

She didn't answer. Instead she looked wryly at her glass,
as if it were an old friend she'd always known would someday turn against her.

"Please, Miss Cartridge. I need help. If you know anything—"

"Why should I help you? Nobody's going to help me."

I remained silent.

"On the other hand, why shouldn't I tell you? It can't
make any real difference to me now. Why shouldn't I make
Craig and Marcia's kid a present? Call it a good-bye present.
I always liked them, even though Craig could be a devil at
times, and Marcia was a soft-hearted fool."

The pulse in my throat beat suffocatingly hard. What was
she going to tell me? I thought of what Steven Carr had said
about her. Thinking it was just the fantasy of a disappointed

and envious man, I had given little weight to his suspicion. But what if this doomed woman, seated only three feet from me, was the one who had stabbed my father to death?

"We were all drinking that night," she said, "but I guess I'd had more than the others. I usually did—do. Anyway, I realized all of a sudden I'd better have some coffee. I went back to the kitchen, but I couldn't find the coffeepot, so I went out the back door. I thought fresh air might do me some good. I went around the corner of the house and leaned against the wall.

"After a minute I realized somebody was in the study with Craig. They were quarreling. I guess nobody across the hall from the study heard it, what with the piano and the singing and all, but out there, with the study doors open onto the terrace, I could hear it.

"Suddenly a man came out on the terrace and then came toward me, almost running. I guess he couldn't see me, there against the wall, because he ran right into me with his shoulder. He swore, and then muttered something—maybe some sort of apology—and then went on around to the back of the house. I followed him far enough to see him climbing that little path by the garage up to the moor. There was no moon that night, but there were lots of stars. I recognized him, all right."

I thought of that dental appointment that had been, not for Monday afternoon, but early Monday morning. "Richard Coventry," I said.

She stared at me. "Who? Oh, yes, I remember him. He wasn't anywhere near the place. He'd gone down to London the day before. Said he had a Monday appointment with his doctor, or somebody. No, the man who ran into me was that neighbor, James MacKelvin, the one who'd been quarreling with the Deverons for years about some lousy sheep."

I felt nothing at all for a moment. Then my stomach tightened into a sick knot. Please, God, I prayed, let her be lying. Not James MacKelvin. Not Michael's father.

Michael. Only about twenty-four hours ago, there beside the pond in Kew Gardens, he had asked to marry him. And I had returned to the hotel to stare at the ceiling of my room and think of lying in Michael's arms in some room of that beautiful old house, with the loch beneath our window stretching calm in the moonlight. Cluny Cartridge said, "What's the matter? You're white as a sheet. Maybe you'd better go lie down."

"It's all right." I gulped some of my drink, and it helped a little. "Go on."

"Well, you've got to understand that in those days I was flat broke. Me, Cluny Cartridge, who'd had stars and directors and even studio heads eating out of my hand." She stared at her glass for a moment and then said, "But to hell with all that. Anyway, the next morning, after the police had taken Marcia away, I walked down to the village. That wasn't too long a walk for me in those days, even with a hangover. From the call box there on the high street I phoned James MacKelvin and told him that he and I had something to talk about. The police had already been there for his statement, I found out later. Apparently that had been enough to scare him stiff. Anyway, he didn't even try to get out of seeing me.

"He suggested that I walk outside the village, so he could pick me up and we could drive someplace where nobody would see us. I said no. I wasn't going to risk his driving up some glen and sticking a knife into *me*. Finally we arranged that I'd go to the little side parlor of the pub, and he'd walk in, and we'd meet as if by accident.

"It was still early. The pub had just opened, and he and I had the side parlor all to ourselves. I asked him if he'd told the police he'd been at Deveron Hall the night before, and he said no. Then I told him that if he'd deposit five thousand pounds to my credit, under the name of Helen Carewe, in a London bank, I'd forget all about seeing him run out of the study."

I thought of them facing each other in that pub, the ex-columnist grimly determined to make something of this chance that had come her way, and the Scottish aristocrat and fancier of seventeenth-century poetry, no doubt clutching at whatever dignity remained to him.

Cluny Cartridge poured herself another drink, and then went on, "He said he saw no reason to pay me. 'Marsden was alive when I left him,' he said. I asked why in that case he had told the police he hadn't been there at all, and he said something about how he couldn't stand the sordidness of being mixed up in a murder case. I told him he'd find everything a lot more sordid if the police found out that he had lied to them.

"He paid up, all right. Two days after I opened an account in the name of Helen Carewe in a London bank, he sent his check. I hadn't intended to ask for more money. I figured that with five thousand pounds I could get some decent clothes and a decent apartment, and then find some English newspaper or magazine to hire me as a columnist. You know how it is, or maybe you don't, but anyway, nobody wants to give you a job if you look as if you really need one.

"But it didn't work out that way. Maybe part of the trouble was the damn telly. Already the stars were going on talk shows. People felt that since they could have the stars right in their living rooms, so to speak, they could know all about them without reading some columnist.

"In a few months I'd spent the five thousand pounds." Defensiveness came into her bitter face. "I had two choices. I could go back to living off a small annuity I'd bought in my palmy days, in some bed-sitter with a gas plate behind a curtain. Or I could hit James MacKelvin up again.

"I called him long distance, and said I wanted more money. He didn't argue for long. After all, as soon as he'd paid me that first time, he was thoroughly on the hook. When I'd run through the second check he sent, I told him we'd have to have a permanent arrangement—a check every four months. That's the way it has been ever since."

Did Michael know? Of course he did. He helped manage his father's business affairs. He could not possibly be ignorant of a sizable yearly drain from the MacKelvin estate.

"Well, there it is. I don't care what you do with it. I don't care if I'm charged with blackmail. I have enough money to keep myself out of jail for the next few months, and after that it won't matter."

In my own pain and bitterness, I brushed aside the knowledge that this woman was dying. "And you've kept silent all these years, living like this"—I gestured around the room—"while my mother—"

"Now wait a minute! If you'd been there that night, you'd have known that Marcia was out of her mind, off somewhere where she didn't see us or hear us, or feel us when we touched her. She was slated for a mental hospital, no matter what I told or didn't tell."

Perhaps. Discovering a beloved husband knifed to death might send any woman out of her mind for a time. But one thing I felt sure of. If the court had not believed she was the one who wielded that knife, and if she herself had not become convinced that she had, she would not have spent the last eighteen years in confinement. And in all probability neither she nor the court would have believed her guilty if they had known about that visit from an infuriated James MacKelvin.

"Anyway," Cluny Cartridge said, "I've told you now. And I didn't have to tell you, did I? Well, did I?"

"No," I conceded, "you didn't have to tell me." But I found it impossible to express any sort of gratitude.

"What are you going to do now?"

"Go back to Scotland." Back to my mother and Richard Coventry, so that the three of us could decide what to do about James MacKelvin.

I said, "Would you be willing to give a sworn, written statement of all you've told me today?"

After a moment she shrugged. "Why not? What have I got to lose?"

I did manage then to say, "Thank you."

"And anyway, I'd like to see that high-nosed old bastard get his. Every time I've talked to him, he's managed to let me know, without saying it, that to him I'm so much dirt under his feet. And not just because I was bleeding him. He made me feel that to him someone like me was just naturally so much dirt."

I stood up and placed my glass on the little table. "I'd better go now."

"I feel a bit wobbly. Mind letting yourself out?"

"Not at all."

Lovey woke up before I reached the door. Even when I was halfway to the elevator, I could still hear his spiteful yapping.

Blind to everything around me, I rode in a bus back to Sloane Square. It now seemed incredible that I, a normally intelligent person, had been fatuous enough to believe that Michael was sincere. Why should he, the heir to that beautiful house, the descendant of all those men and women in the portraits—why should a man like that want to marry an obscure American schoolteacher, especially one with my background?

His lovemaking and his proposal had been a tactic designed to keep me from finding out what had actually happened at Deveron Hall that night. How the tactic was to work, I did not know. Would he actually have married me? Perhaps, if he had felt it to be necessary. He might hope that after a few months as his wife, it would not matter too much if I learned the truth. By then I would have become a MacKelvin, willing to protect the MacKelvin name at any cost, even that of letting my mother live out her life believing that she had killed the man she loved.

"Sloane Square," the conductor said. "Didn't you say you wanted to get off at Sloane Square?"

When I entered the little lobby a few minutes later, I found the manager seated at her desk. She said, "Good afternoon, Miss Marsden." Then: "Are you all right? You don't look well."

"I'm all right. I'm leaving tomorrow."

"We'll be sorry to lose you. Are you returning to Scotland?"

"Yes, I don't suppose you know what train I should take. I want to make a connection with an Inverness train."

I didn't know how I would get from Inverness to Harlaig and Deveron Hall. Probably it would be best to phone Richard Coventry from the Inverness station and ask him to drive down to get me.

"I think there's a noon train from Euston Station for Glasgow. But I don't know whether it connects with an Inverness train. Better to call the station."

"Yes, I'll call them."

Chapter
Sixteen

It was raining when I left the train in Glasgow late the next afternoon, and still raining when, after an hour's wait in the echoing station, I boarded a slow local for Inverness. Most of the time as the train moved north and west, I did not look at the few other passengers in the second-class coach—a sleeping old man, a woman knitting a child's pink sweater, and four shaggy-haired youths talking in some incomprehensible dialect, perhaps Lancashire, as they played cards on the table between their seats. Instead I stared at my ghostly reflection in the windowpane, and the rain slashing down like silver needles against the gathering dark outside.

I tried not to think of Michael and of what I would say to him when next we met. First things first. I must think of how to tell my mother what I had learned. Just how do you tell a woman that, if two people had not suppressed the truth, she might never have been charged with her husband's murder? Oh, she would feel relief at this evidence of her own innocence. But at the same time, surely, the thought of those wasted years would bring her a bitterness whose depths I did not want to imagine.

Better, I decided, to tell Richard Coventry first, and then work out between us what we would say to her, and when. After that we would have to get Cluny Cartridge's sworn statement. Probably Richard would say that I should have managed to get something in writing before I left her apartment. But I had been too eager to get away from that woman with her ravaged face, and away from all that luxury which, in a way, had been created at the cost of eighteen years of my mother's life.

The train slowed. The woman across the aisle from me began to bundle up her knitting. I asked, "Is this Inverness?"

"It is, dearie."

Our coach slid past the few people waiting on the rain-wet station platform, upturned faces scanning the train windows. A woman with two sleepy-looking little girls. A man in a yellow slicker and a sou'wester hat.

And Michael, his face lighting up when he saw me.

As the train slid past him, I thought, in a kind of panic, I can't see him now. I had an impulse to run back along the train and leave it by the rear coach, in the hope of evading him. But no, I had to face him sooner or later. It might as well be now.

When I descended the train steps, he was waiting. He took my suitcase and then, before I could turn my head away, leaned down and kissed me. "Hello, darling." Then, frowning: "What is it? You're awfully pale."

Fleetingly I was aware that his face, too, had a strained look. "I'm tired, that's all. How did you know I was on—"

"I phoned your hotel in London this afternoon. The woman there told me that you'd probably be on tonight's Inverness train. Are you hungry? You look as if you could use some food."

"I had dinner on the Glasgow train."

"Then we'd better start. It will be slow driving. The radio

says this is one of the heaviest rainfalls Scotland has had in years."

We left the station and walked along an arcade to where he had parked the Land Rover. He said, as we drove through the town, "Did you get to the hairdressers?"

"Yes."

"Your hair looks lovely. But then, it looked lovely before."

It was too much of an effort to think of a reply to that, and so I made none. After a moment he said, in an altered tone, "There's something very wrong. What is it, darling?"

My throat felt as if a metal band had tightened around it. I knew what he was now, a hypocrite and a trickster, intent only upon protecting James MacKelvin. Why did I find it so hard to tell him I knew, so hard to say the few sentences that would keep him from calling me darling ever again?

I said, "I told you. I'm just tired."

"Then why don't you curl up in the corner and try to sleep?"

I took the coward's way out. "All right."

Huddled with closed eyes in the corner of the seat, I listened to the steady hum of the engine and the drum of rain on the roof. Now and then lights glowed against my eyelids, and I knew we must be passing through some small village. Then there were no more lights. From the way Michael handled the car, slowing frequently and then shifting gears to drive with a splashing sound across some low spot, I knew that we must have left the paved road for a dirt one. I heard him lower the window a little on his side, letting in cool air and the smell of heather. It reminded me of the day I had met him on the moors, with the bracken and the rosy heather stretching all around us.

At last he touched my shoulder gently. "Lisa?" I sat up.

"I hate to wake you," he said, "but I must. We're near Harlaig now, and I have to talk to you."

"I wasn't asleep." My voice sounded toneless to my own ears. "What do you want to tell me?"

"That I'm not taking you to Deveron Hall. I'm taking you to my house."

I looked at his face, pale and set in the upward striking light from the dashboard. "What on earth are you talking about?"

"Listen to me, Lisa. Listen carefully. You're not safe with your mother."

"Not safe with—" Sudden rage swept through me. "I told you what Dr. Crandall said about her. You didn't dispute it. You reached your hand across the table and said, 'I'm glad!'"

"I know. I believed then that he knew what he was talking about. Now I know he was wrong. Wait until I get through this."

There was a water-filled dip in the road ahead. He guided the car through it. Then he said, "I told my father this morning that we were going to be married. He seemed upset at first, as I knew he would. I've already told you why. Then he went out fishing. He must have thought it over while he was out there by himself, because when he came back—"

"Just what," I asked thickly, "has all this to do with my mother?"

"Listen, please listen. He wanted to send some trout over to your mother—sort of a first gesture of reconciliation between her family and ours, I suppose. I took the basket of fish over. Your mother answered the door. I said I was taking the trout around to the back, and she said no, I could give it to her, and just then the phone rang.

"It was my father, asking for me. He wanted me to write out a recipe for trout with wine sauce that our family has used for years, and give it to your mother."

He stopped speaking. I stared straight ahead at the silvery slashes of rain falling through the headlights' beams. Then he said, "She took a pencil and paper from the phone table's drawer and gave it to me. You know that mirror on the wall above the phone table?"

"Yes."

"I was writing down the directions my father gave me when I happened to look up into the mirror. I saw her staring at my back. If I've ever seen murderous venom in a human face, it was in hers. I don't know why. Probably because she never wanted you to come here. Probably because she feels I'm part of the reason you're staying here. Anyway, I have no doubt that if she'd had a knife and thought she could get away with it, she'd have plunged it between my shoulder blades. I gave her the recipe, went home, and telephoned your hotel."

I said, in a voice I would not have recognized as my own, "Liar. Filthy liar."

He didn't answer, just drove ahead to a turnoff, and stopped there. He said, turning to me, "God, Lisa, do you think I wanted to tell you this? But I had to."

"Liar!" I said again. "I don't know why you're trying to make me afraid of my own mother. I don't know why you want to take me to your house. But I know it has nothing to do with *my* safety. It's your father you're worried about."

"Lisa, for God's sake—"

"If you want to talk to me about someone, talk to me about Helen Carewe."

If I'd ever clung to a faint hope that Michael knew nothing of his father's relationship with that bitter-eyed woman down in London, that hope was gone now. Michael's face was both stunned and appalled.

He said, "How is it you know about her?"

"Don't worry," I said in that same thick voice. "I'll tell you. But first I want you to tell me this. How long have you known your father was sending money to that woman?"

"Six years, perhaps seven."

"And you did nothing about it. You let my mother stay in that place all those years, thinking that *she* was the one who—"

"Lisa!"

He reached out for me. I struck his hand away. "All right," he said, withdrawing into his own corner. "Just tell me about it."

I told him about my visit to Cluny Cartridge. As I spoke, I saw a growing bleakness in his face. "And you *knew* about her and your father," I said.

"I knew he was sending money regularly to a Helen Carewe. But I didn't know why, and I didn't know that Helen Carewe was that—gossip columnist. I thought she was just some woman he'd become involved with at some time in the past, and felt responsible for."

I asked, bitterly skeptical, "And not a blackmailer?"

"The thought of blackmail crossed my mind a few times."

"But you dismissed it. A MacKelvin couldn't possibly do anything that could put himself in the hands of a blackmailer, could he?"

When he finally spoke, he sounded tired. "Lisa, what are you going to do?"

"Get a sworn statement from Cluny Cartridge and turn it over to the police."

He said in that same tired voice, "My father's not a murderer. I see now that he must have been at Deveron Hall that night, and had a quarrel with Craig Marsden. But he didn't kill him. You'll be causing pain and humiliation to an old man whose only crime was family pride and cowardice."

"If those were his only crimes, he doesn't have much to worry about, does he? He won't be charged with anything except lying to the police."

There was pain in his face. "Don't do this. It won't change what's already happened to your mother. Don't do it. I love you, Lisa."

"I don't believe you. And even if I did, it wouldn't stop me. If there's anything I can do to clear my mother, in her own mind and everyone else's, I'm going to do it."

His eyes went cold. As we stared at each other, the memory of a poem flashed through my head, a poem about a man and a woman who had thought that their love would always be a green, growing thing—until, in November, they had looked at each other "across the blackened vine." It was not November, but we faced each other across a dead and blackened vine, all right. I could almost see it lying there between us.

He said, "At least don't go to Deveron Hall tonight."

"Let you take me to your house, so you can tell me more lies, and maybe persuade me to forget what Cluny Cartridge told me? It won't work, Michael. I don't believe that —that you saw what you say you did in my mother's face. And I'm going to Deveron Hall, even if I have to get out of this car and walk."

Without speaking, he started the car and drove on. We went through Harlaig. It was completely dark except for a light shining from the pub window. Apparently it was earlier than I had thought. I glanced at my watch. Still not eleven. We drove on, over the bridge that was now awash with an inch or so of water, and then turned onto the long drive up to Deveron Hall.

Still neither of us spoke. I wondered what he was thinking. Probably about Cluny Cartridge. He must have some hope that he could persuade her not to make that statement. It was a vain hope, it seemed to me. How could one either bribe or effectively threaten a dying woman? Too, he must be thinking about what legal defense could be made for his father, if worst came to worst.

He stopped the car in front of the portico. Dim light shone through the glass doors. The window of my mother's upstairs room also was lighted. Otherwise the house was dark. He said, turning to me, "For the last time, don't stay here."

I reached back and hauled my light suitcase over to the front seat. "Good-bye, Michael." I unlatched the door and got out. He drove around the loop in the drive and then headed downhill.

For a second or two I stood there in the downpour, watching those red taillights, and feeling regret and a wild, irrepressible longing. I had known him and loved him for such a short time. Surely it would not take long to get over loving him. But I was afraid it would.

I turned, climbed the steps, and went into the house. The study door stood partly open. I walked to it. The room was unlighted, but I saw what I had hoped to see—the red glow of a banked fire in the hearth. Leaving my suitcase in the hall, I went into the study, turned on the light, and held my cold hands to the fire's warmth.

My mother, evidently, was still awake. Was Richard Coventry? Whether he was or not, I could not talk it over with him tonight. I felt too utterly bleak and broken.

I was still standing there when the phone in the hall rang.

After a hesitant moment, I went out and picked it up. The voice of a male operator said, "I have a trunk call from London for Miss Lisa Marsden."

I heard buzzing sounds on the line, and then a single click. "This is Lisa Marsden."

"Thank you, Miss Marsden. Go ahead, sir."

A warm, remembered voice said, "This is Dr. Crandall, Miss Marsden. I am sorry to call you so late, but when I telephoned your hotel this afternoon, I was told you had left for Scotland by train. I estimated that you should have reached home by now. I hope you hadn't retired."

"No. I've been here only about ten minutes."

"The purpose of my call is this, Miss Marsden. This morning I realized that there was something important which I had forgotten to tell you when you were at the hospital. Perhaps I had repressed the thought of it because I realized it would be painful to you. But it's important, and you should know about it."

My heart was beating hard with the memory of Michael's voice, describing a certain look on my mother's face. "What is it, Dr. Crandall?"

"If your mother appears severely depressed, get medical help at once. You see, what I did not tell you was that five years ago she tried to commit suicide. She slit her wrists. Perhaps you haven't noticed the scars. They are quite faint."

More buzzings on the storm-lashed line, mingled with the drumming of my blood in my ears. Scars. That woman on the moor, with the sleeves of her bedraggled gray sweater falling back, revealing the thin scars on her wrists. That woman to whom I had delivered that cardboard box, a box too small to hold regular glasses, only large enough for granny glasses—a box which I realized now had held neither.

That woman who had tried her best, just as Michael had a few minutes ago, to get me to leave this place.

I said mechanically, "Yes, I've noticed the scars. But thank you, Dr. Crandall."

"Not at all. Good night, Miss Marsden."

He hung up. Then, as I stood there frozen, the phone still held to my ear, I heard another click, as if somewhere in this house an extension phone had been replaced in its cradle.

Chapter
Seventeen

I too hung up, aware of a bead of cold sweat rolling down my side. There was an extension phone in that room at the top of the stairs. I'd seen it. Had she really been listening in, or was it the storm that twice had made that clicking sound on the line? In either case, I had to get to my mother right now. Get to her, and get us both out of this house.

I went up the stairs quickly and softly, keeping close to the wall to avoid that creaking midsection of each step. Amber lights burned in the wall sockets in the upstairs hall— dim lights, but strong enough so that I could not see whether or not more light seeped out from beneath the closed door of that corner room. Swiftly I went on down the hall to the door opposite my own room. At my right, I could hear wind-driven rain beating against the window above the rear stairwell.

I didn't knock. I just went in. The room was in darkness except for an arc of light from the half-open bathroom door. As I moved forward, the scent of sandalwood soap became stronger. I stopped in the bathroom doorway. Wearing an old blue robe, she stood bent over the washbasin. Her startled face swung toward me. It was white in its frame of gray curls, and ravaged by the years and by sorrow, but it was still the gentle face of my mother.

With terror leaping into her green eyes, she gave a little

cry and reached up toward a glass wall shelf at one side of the basin.

I caught her hand. "Don't bother with the dark glasses, Mother, or the contact lenses either. Just get dressed. We've got to get out of here."

Her face crumpled. "Oh, Lisa! Oh, my baby! Why did you come back? How I prayed you wouldn't come back."

"Mother, get dressed! If you've got boots and a raincoat, put them on. We're going to have to walk, and it's terrible out."

She seized my arms. "Lisa, go away before either of them find out that you know. They'll kill you, Lisa. They already tried to. They did something to the brakes on your car."

"It's too late. I'm afraid Amy already knows I've found out."

She gave a whimper. "Then go right now, before Richard Coventry gets back from Inverness. They won't do anything to me. They *need* me. All they'll do to me, if I don't do as they say, is to see to it that I'm sent back to that place."

"Nobody is going to send you anywhere," I said fiercely. "Nobody is going to do any cruel thing to you ever again. Now get dressed. And hurry!"

Her defenses collapsed. I saw their collapse in her great green eyes. "All right, darling. I'll hurry."

I left her room, softly closing the door behind me, and crossed to my own room. I switched on the light with one hand as I swung back the door with the other. Then I ran to the wardrobe, knelt, and tugged at the big drawer set in its base. Dampness had swollen the wood. When the drawer finally came loose, it made a rending noise. No matter. All that mattered was getting out of here, while there was still only one of them to try to stop us.

I took my boots, black leather ones, from the drawer,

carried them over to the bed, sat down, and kicked off my citified brown kid pumps. Thank God I'd put on warm clothing, a dark red skirt and sweater, in my London hotel room that morning. I need not worry that I, at least, would find the stormy night too cold.

I was reaching for a boot when I heard, from across the hall, the sound of a key turning in a lock. I shot to my feet.

She came in, a little woman with dyed red hair, wearing the familiar black pants and black turtleneck, and moving as soundlessly as a cat in felt-soled green house slippers. She had a gun in her hand.

"Just sit down," she said.

I sank back onto the bed. She sat down in a straight chair and, with the gun leveled at me, looked at me from calm brown eyes.

I said, past the pulse hammering in the hollow of my throat, "Hello, Mrs. Harnish. Or is it Mrs. Coventry?"

"It is. Richard and I were married in London eight months ago."

Eight months ago, soon after she began to visit my mother at the hospital. Fleetingly I wondered, although it did not matter, whether they had made their plans concerning my mother before or after their marriage.

"Now we're just going to sit here quietly until Richard gets back from Inverness and we can decide what to do about you. It won't be long. A few hours ago he phoned to say he'd had to have the windscreen wiper on his car fixed. But he'll be home by midnight at the latest."

No sound from behind that locked door across the hall. I pictured my mother pacing the floor, or perhaps huddled in a chair, mute with terror. Despite my own fear, the thought brought me a surge of rage.

I said, "You're after her money, of course."

"Of course. Next week the lawyers who have held her estate in trust all these years will be up here. In their presence, she'll sign over power of attorney to my husband and me."

"She won't be wearing brown contact lenses that day, will she?"

Amy smiled. "A red wig I bought for her in London, but no contacts. And I won't be wearing mine, either." Her smile vanished. "I hate the damned things. If I wear them more than a few hours, my eyelids swell."

"Where did you get them, anyway? I never heard of colored contact lenses."

"They're called cosmetic lenses. Theatrical people sometimes use them. Before we left London, we took Marcia to this London firm which supplies them. I'd told her that I intended to get contacts, and I persuaded her to be measured for a pair of them too."

"Of course you didn't tell her that both pairs were to be colored."

"Of course not. I didn't even give her her lenses until after we brought her up here. We didn't tell her any of our plans until she was here." Her face darkened. "Then, just a few days before you showed up, the clumsy fool knocked one of her lenses off a shelf into the washbasin and it went down the drain. I'm sure it was an accident. She's been too scared to try any tricks. But by the time Richard got the drainpipe off and found the lens, it was all out of shape and useless. I had to phone London for another pair."

The gun hadn't wavered, nor had she looked away from me for even an instant. But she would, I told myself fervently, she would, if her husband stayed away much longer. And in the meantime, I had to keep her talking.

A gust of wind blew rain against the window so violently

that the sound was like that of flung gravel. I said, raising my voice, "But why did you bother with the hair dye and the contact lenses?"

"Now, Lisa! A bright girl like you ought to be able to figure that out. We had to convince the locals that Marcia Deveron Marsden had not only returned to her old home, but was completely free to move about—go shopping, collect the mail, and so on. Otherwise, someone might have taken it into his head to write or phone her lawyers that there was something funny going on at Deveron Hall. People saw the man and woman who'd come up here with her, some busybody might tell them, but nobody ever saw *her.*"

Another burst of wind-driven rain struck the window. She waited until the noise lessened and then said, "But of course we couldn't have Marcia running around the village and giving orders to Jennie—not when we'd told her she was going to have to sign that power of attorney. True, she was too scared of us to tell anyone, but that was just it. People would realize she was scared of something, and begin to wonder. So for a while I had to be Marcia, and Marcia had to be my poor sick cousin Amy, who never wanted to see anybody."

I looked at the lined face in its frame of dyed hair. Even allowing for the fact that she was an actress, how had she been able to convince me that she was my mother? Perhaps I had not been deceived, deep in my subconscious. Perhaps that was why, the first night I came here, the word "mother" had stuck in my throat.

I said, "Aren't you overlooking something? What's to prevent her, once she's in the same room with her lawyers, from telling them all about it?"

"We've warned her what will happen if she tries that. We'll tell her lawyers, more in sorrow than in anger, that she's had a relapse, that in fact she'd tried to attack me with a knife the night before. We'd hoped to be able to take care of her, we'll tell them, but maybe since she's suffering these wild delusions about us, it's better that she go back to the hospital."

"I see. And after she signs and the lawyers are gone, what then? Does she believe that you'll give her some of her own money and let her go away?"

Amy said shortly, "Something like that."

"But what will you really do to her?" Despite my efforts to keep calm, my voice shook.

She didn't answer.

"Well? Will you arrange a little accident? You two are good at that, aren't you?"

For the first time, she showed real anger. "Shut up! Why did you ever come here? Certainly you'd had no encouragement to come."

"No, I didn't. And when I got here my dear mama, in her green contacts and dyed hair, didn't seem very glad to see me, and my dear steppapa-to-be made a pass at me, and then either you or he put a dead squirrel in my bureau drawer—"

"I told Richard that wouldn't work. But he thought you might think that I—I mean your mother—had done it. He thought you'd conclude that if your mother was still loopy enough to do a thing like that, Deveron Hall was not going to be a pleasant place to stay."

"I thought Jennie had done it."

She smiled. "I'll tell Richard that, just to show him how wrong he can be."

"And he didn't have much better luck when he messed up the brakes on my car, did he?"

Again that flash of anger. "Shut up."

I said, leaning forward, "You killed my father, didn't you?"

"Stay where you are! Straighten up!"

I straightened. After a moment she said in a calm voice, "All right, I killed him. If you know that, maybe you won't get any bright ideas about trying to rush me when I've got a gun in my hand."

"Why? Why did you kill him?"

"Because he was throwing me over!" Her mouth twisted. "I had thought he was going to divorce Marcia and marry me. Lord knows he'd seemed crazy about me for a while down in London. But when I came up here with the other house guests, I saw his feelings had changed, maybe because he and Marcia had been having so many rows about me. And then, that last night—"

She went on speaking, swiftly and bitterly, her voice drowned out now and then by the wind-driven rain. After dinner that summer night eighteen years before—that uncomfortable dinner, with my mother neither looking at my father nor speaking to him—he had shut himself up in the study. Amy went with the other guests and my mother into the drawing room.

"Marcia was laughing and talking and dancing with the two men, Steven Carr and that old character actor who had played her father in the film. I forget his name. Anyway, he's dead now. I guess she was trying to make up for being so silent at dinner. And I too was trying to act as if I was having a good time. Then that bitchy Steven Carr made some crack at me about actresses who try to sleep their way to the top. I felt I hated all of them, not just Marcia, but all of them, and couldn't stand being with them another minute."

She had gone up to her room and undressed for bed.

Then, desperate at the thought that the house party would break up the next morning, and that she might never see my father again, she had decided to find out, once and for all, just where she stood with him. She had put a robe on over her nightgown, gone down the back stairs, and circled around to the terrace entrance to the study.

"He was already sore when I came in to talk to him. Some neighbor had been there, quarreling over some money he claimed the Deverons had owed him for years and years. I told him I had to know where I stood. He said something evasive and I lost my temper, and I began crying and calling him all the names I could think of, while he just got calmer and calmer. Finally he said, 'Amy, you're a fool. Whatever gave you the idea that I'd divorce Marcia—*Marcia!*—to marry a dime-a-dozen little tramp like you? And now if you'll excuse me, I have to make a phone call.'"

My father had turned in his swivel chair toward the phone. Amy picked up the paperknife and stabbed him in the back, and then, when he tried to get up, several times in the throat, and then in the back again. Then she stood there and looked at him, slumped over his desk with the knife handle protruding from his back.

"I realized he was dead, and that I had blood all down the front of my robe. I went out the terrace door and around to the kitchen and up the back stairs. I didn't see anyone. In my room I stripped off my robe and gown and wadded them in one corner of my suitcase. Then I put on the same dress I'd been wearing earlier and went down to the drawing room. I could tell everyone had had a lot to drink by then, so much so that even if any of them had noticed me leaving, they wouldn't be able to say for sure whether I'd been gone five minutes or half an hour.

"After a while Marcia left the room. We didn't know then

that she'd crossed the hall to go into the study. We didn't know it until Steven Carr went out into the hall for one reason or another. He let out a yell, and we all rushed out to him.

"Marcia, the damn fool, had pulled the knife out of Craig's back. She was standing there with her face a blank, and the knife still in her hand, and blood down the front of her dress. Cluny Cartridge, a broken-down Hollywood columnist who was there, and this young actress named Connie something-or-other took Marcia up to her room. Then Steven Carr called the police."

Evidently her arm had grown tired. The gun, although still pointed at me, now rested on her knee.

I said, "You hated my mother even before your affair with my father, didn't you?"

Her eyes blazed. "Of course I hated her. I hated her even when we were children. It wasn't fair," she went on in a brooding voice, "that this should be her home, something her father just let me share. If my father had been born first, it would have been my house. And she had everything else, too. Even at ten she was beautiful. And everyone but me seemed to like her. She was the most popular girl at our school.

"Later on it was even worse. We both wanted to be actresses, but when we went down to London to try out that repertory theater, it was her they chose. She had to talk to the manager for several weeks before he agreed to let me join the company, and even then I got only walk-on parts.

"After she went to Hollywood and married Craig, I kept writing her that I'd like him to get the studio to sign me, and she kept writing back that she was trying to persuade him to. Even when they came to London to make that film, it was Marcia who finally convinced him I'd be all right for a small part."

She had lowered her gaze to stare moodily at the gun. "God, how sick I was of it. Her always the Lady Bountiful, and me always—"

I picked up one of my boots and hurled it straight into her face.

Chapter
Eighteen

She tried to dodge. Her chair tilted. As I launched myself
toward her from the bed's edge, the gun went off, and I
heard a thin whine close to my ear that might have been the
bullet's passage. Then the woman and the chair and I, all in
a tangle, crashed to the floor.

With my right forearm forcing her chin back, she glared
up at me. My left hand reached for her wrist, found it and
twisted, trying to force her to drop the gun. Her finger must
have been pulling the trigger spasmodically, because the
gun went off three more times, or perhaps four. Through the
explosions I could hear my mother across the hall screaming
out her terror and despair.

Amy not only had held onto the gun. She had worked her
other hand free from beneath my weight and now had it
raised, taloned fingers bent to rake my eyes. I flung my head
back to avoid those sharp nails. My own movement must
have thrown me off balance and for an instant loosened my
grip on her wrist, because suddenly—for all that I was
younger, taller, heavier—she had broken free of me and was
starting to stand up. With despair I saw that before I too
could scramble to my feet, she would send a bullet crashing
into me. My hands shot out, grasped the thin ankles, jerked.
She went over backward. I heard the report of the gun and

then, almost simultaneously, the hollow sound of her head striking the floor.

I knelt beside her. Eyes dazed, she tried to raise her head. I grasped her sweater front with my left hand and, with my right fist, hit her on the chin as hard as I could. She went limp. I lowered her head to the floor and then, aware of pain in my own right hand, took the gun from her unresisting one. Then I felt for her pulse. It was still beating.

When I stood up, I looked bitterly down at the still face, wishing I were capable of hitting her over the head with the gun butt, just to make sure she stayed out for a while. But I had no idea of how hard I could hit her without killing her.

Silence across the hall now. I could picture my mother crumpled on the bed or on the floor, sure that by now I was dead. But I couldn't go to her yet. I laid the gun on the bed and then, with hands that were shaking and clumsy, took two pairs of panty hose and a blue triangular scarf from the bureau. I forced the scarf between her teeth and tied it at the back of her head. I bound her ankles with one pair of panty hose, turned her over, and bound her hands behind her back with the other pair. Then, hands under her armpits, I dragged her into the bathroom and left her there on the tiled floor. There was no way of locking her inside. All I could do was close the door. But even so, pray God it would take Richard Coventry a while to find her and take the gag from her mouth.

I crossed the hall. Amy had left the heavy old skeleton key in the lock. So that my mother would know it was I outside her door, I called "Mother?" Then I turned the key in the lock.

She sat on the edge of the bed, green eyes enormous in her ashen face. Before Amy locked her in, apparently my mother had had time to put on her plaid skirt and gray sweater. But she was still shoeless and stockingless. She said in a voice as high and thin as a child's, "I thought—"

"I know. But I'm not. Finish dressing. Hurry!"

She stood up. "The police. Shouldn't we—"

"There are no police nearer than Dingwall, except for an old constable in the village." By that time I was kneeling on the floor beside the wardrobe, hoping to find boots or galoshes in its drawer. "And it would take him a long time to get here on a night like this. Probably too long."

From her swift intake of breath I knew that she had understood me. Richard Coventry might be here at any moment. But before we left the house, I would try to phone the constable, and Lochnail too. Had Michael had time to get home? Swiftly I glanced at my watch. Almost midnight. Yes, surely he would be home.

She had no boots, no galoshes. I snatched up the worn black oxfords and carried them to her. She was pulling a stocking onto her leg. "Wear a sweater," I said, "and a raincoat, or the heaviest coat you've got. And wear a head scarf."

Reaching for the other stocking beside her on the bed, she looked up at me and nodded.

I went back across the hall and looked into the bathroom. Amy still lay motionless, eyes closed.

The thought of her aged Bentley out there in the garage crossed my mind. If I had its keys— But I had no idea where she kept them, and I dared not risk taking time to make a search. I shut the bathroom door, and gathered up the flung boot and its mate and put them on. I slipped into my white plastic raincoat and dropped the gun into its right-hand pocket. Then I tied a brown woolen head scarf under my chin, switched off the light, and, closing the door behind me, went back to my mother.

She was fully dressed now, in an old tan coat and black head scarf. Whether from shock or a supreme effort of will, she seemed quite calm. "Where are we going?"

"To the village. We'll find someone to help us."

We went along the hall and down the front staircase. At its foot I said, "Wait. I'm going to phone—"

I broke off. From outside had come the whine of a car, in low gear, ascending the muddy drive leading up from the road.

My heart hammered against my chest. No chance to get past him down the hillside.

I had the gun. Should I try to take him by surprise, order him up to my mother's room, and lock him in?

Then, cold and almost sick with dismay, I realized that perhaps the gun was useless. How many shots had Amy fired during our struggle? Five? Six? Perhaps the gun's chamber was empty. And I had neither the time, nor the knowledge to break the gun open and find out.

Try to bluff him with a perhaps empty gun? I couldn't risk it. He would probably see the truth in my face.

That whining sound was louder now. I seized her hand, drew her at a half run back down the hall, through the baize door into the utter darkness beyond. Thankfully I remembered that the door at the end of the hall and the kitchen's back door were in a straight line, with no furniture in between. Now if only the back door was unlocked—

It was. I opened the screen door, drew her outside. Rain-laden wind tore at our bodies, wrenched the screen door from my hand. It banged shut. Had he, through the storm and the sound of the Buick's engine, heard that banging door? Even if he had, there was no help for it.

I led her across the graveled space in front of the garage's dark bulk to the foot of that steep little path. "Go ahead of me." We started scrambling up it, feet slipping in the mud, hands clutching at the gorse bushes and heather at either side of the path. Would he stop in the front of the portico or drive back to the garage? With near despair I realized that if his headlights touched my wet white raincoat, it would shine like a beacon.

I looked up. Already his headlights, angling up the steep drive, shone dimly on the old cedar tree at the top of the path. When he reached the terrace on which the house stood, his headlights would sweep downward—

"Wait!" I squeezed past her on the path, scrambled the rest of the way to the top, and flung myself full length on the ground. Reaching my arms down toward the white blur that was her face, I said, "Take my hands."

When I felt her hands grasp mine, I raised myself to my knees and drew her onto the moor. "Keep low!" With the rain beating down on us, we moved a few yards farther into the darkness, and then sank to the soggy ground. Even through the sound of the wind and rain, I could hear her labored breathing. "Wait here," I said.

I retraced my steps until I could see the dead cedar, a deeper black against the darkness. I pressed close to its trunk. Refracted light shone from somewhere near the foot of the path. I could hear the throb of an idling engine. Then the garage door went up with a scraping sound. I heard him drive in, close the garage door. As he went into the house through the back entrance, the wind must have torn the screen door from his grasp, too, because I heard it bang.

I moved back, with the soggy earth sucking at my boots, to her dark, huddled shape. How long would it take him to find Amy? Perhaps twenty minutes, if luck was on our side. And by that time we would be farther away from here, perhaps even far enough.

I said, sinking down beside her, "He's in the house. Rest for a minute more. We've got a long walk ahead."

Her breathing was still labored. "Where are we going?"

"Across the moor to the MacKelvins."

How far was it? My vague estimate was about two miles. Not too far even for a frail woman by daylight and in good weather. But in darkness, and with rain-soaked earth making every step an effort—

Still, it was better than trying to get my mother down that almost vertical path and then safely past the house and down the hillside, when at any moment we might find ourselves bathed by Richard Coventry's headlights. And in all probability, he would be armed. A pair like Richard and Amy Coventry would have more than one gun between them.

I said, "Can you go on now?"

Her white face turned toward me. I saw her nod.

We struck off to our right. My eyes had adjusted to the rainy darkness, at least enough so that I could guide her past boulders, and clumps of gorse, and the larger bulk of the ruined stone hut. We could make it, surely we could. The hard part would be getting down into that glen where James MacKelvin had fished that day, and then up the other side. After that, unless I was mistaken, there would be just moorland to cross.

A few yards beyond the stone hut, my mother gave a little cry, and went down. I crouched beside her. "What is it?"

"My ankle." No need to ask if she were in pain. Her voice told me so. If not actually broken, her ankle was badly sprained.

No hope of getting her down into that glen and up the other side. We would have to spend the night on the moor, praying that Richard and Amy, after they failed to find us anywhere between Deveron Hall and the village, would not come up here looking for us.

That hut back there. Its stone walls would shield us from the worst of the wind, and the broken roof would keep out some of the rain. "We'll go back to the hut."

"No, Lisa. No, darling. You keep on. Get to the MacKelvins. Leave me here. I'll be all right."

All right—when an hour from now, or even sooner, Richard Coventry might be up here with a flashlight and a gun. I said almost angrily, "Don't talk nonsense. Let me help you up. That's right. Now put your arm around my neck."

With her hobbling beside me over the soft and uneven ground, we moved back toward the hut. As we neared it, another realization struck me, making me feel that what I'd been through in the past few hours must have addled my judgment hopelessly. It had been absurd to think that we could reach Lochnail and Michael by crossing the moors. Even without my mother's accident, we would never have gotten across the glen. That footbridge from which James MacKelvin had fished must long since have been buried under the avalanche of water foaming down that narrow canyon.

Chapter
Nineteen

We huddled close together in one corner of the hut under rain that fell almost unimpeded through what remained of the thatched roof. My mother made no complaint, but I could tell from her sharp intake of breath every now and then that pains were shooting through her ankle. I thought of trying to bind it with my rain-soaked head scarf. But in the dark, and completely unskilled in such matters, I might cause her additional pain without doing any good.

"Mother, would you like to talk? Would that help?"

"Yes, darling. Let's talk." She drew another sharp breath. "What happened between you and Amy before that—that gun started going off?"

I hesitated, freshly aware of the weight of that perhaps useless gun in my pocket, and then decided to tell her immediately. "Amy said that she killed my father. She did it in a rage because he'd told her he'd never had any intention of divorcing you to marry her."

She was silent for so long that I began to think she hadn't understood me. And then she began to cry, with great, wrenching sobs that sounded as if they had been stored up for almost a third of her lifetime. I gathered her into my arms.

"Mother, have you really thought all these years that you were the one who—" I stopped.

After a moment she said brokenly, "Everyone said that I did it. And I couldn't remember. But oh, Lisa! I could never understand how I could have done it. I loved him so much."

"I know you did."

"And your father loved me."

Yes, I was sure he had loved her. I could not have been the happy child that I was if I hadn't known that they loved each other.

"I think, if it had come right down to it, that Craig would have given his life for me. What he wouldn't give up, even for me, was other women. And that made it bad, because the only person I wanted was him.

"But oh, Lisa! It's so good to know that it wasn't me who killed him. It's so very good."

She began to cry again. There seemed to be no bitterness in her weeping. Perhaps bitterness over those lost eighteen years would come later. Now there seemed to be no room in her except for a vast and overwhelming relief.

She quieted, finally. Arms still around her, I asked, "How is it you let those two bring you back here?"

"I was so alone when I left the hospital, Lisa. Alone and scared and bewildered. Amy was the only friend I had. She and Richard said that since I had the house, it was only good sense to come up here and wait until the trustee had drawn up the papers transferring everything back into my hands. I didn't want to come here. But I was afraid that if I refused, they might get angry and wash their hands of me. And I'd be alone and friendless in that London that seemed so different. Even the money had changed. No shillings any more. And there were skyscrapers where I remembered rows of little shops, and vacant lots where I remembered buildings. I was always making mistakes about money, and once I got lost—"

I understood. Unsure of herself, afraid that if left alone she might make some "mistake" so serious that she would find herself back in the hospital, she had given in to them.

"After they brought you here, how long was it before they told you why?"

"They told me the next day. They said that once they had the power of attorney, they'd convert everything to cash, send it to a bank in Brazil, and then fly there themselves. But before they left, they said, they'd give me fifty thousand dollars so I could go wherever I chose."

"And you believed them?"

"What else could I do but try to? If I didn't go along with them, they'd say I'd tired to—to kill Amy with a knife. And everyone would have believed that. You see, Lisa," she said quietly, "once you've been in one of those places, people will believe anyone else rather than you."

I found I couldn't speak.

"Besides," she went on, "I think they might have let me go. It would have been less risky than killing me."

Perhaps, I thought, she was right about that. "What did you intend to do?"

"Go back to New York. From your letters I knew where you lived. I thought that if I—made out all right, if I knew I wouldn't be a burden to you, I'd go to you." Her voice gathered speed. "But instead you came here. Oh, Lisa! I've been so terrified. And I didn't dare tell you what was happening. They would have killed you right away if they thought I'd given you any inkling of the truth. I was afraid they would kill you anyway if you didn't leave. And so from the first I tried—"

"It's all right," I soothed. "We're both all right."

We were not all right, of course. We were two women, one frail and temporarily crippled, who at any moment might see, outside the hut's doorway, a flashlight probing the rainy dark. How long had we been up here on the moor? Unable to see my watch, I had no way of knowing. But surely Richard Coventry had found Amy by now, and revived her if she needed reviving, and heard her account of what had happened. Surely they had driven off, hoping to find my mother and me before we could reach the village.

A sudden hope made me catch my breath. After a moment I said, "Wait here."

"Lisa!" She clutched my arm. "What—"

"I'm going as near the house as I safely can. If his car's gone, I'll go in and phone the constable and Michael, so that they can get the police here from Dingwall."

"But what if she's in there waiting—"

"I don't think she'll be in there alone, not when she knows I have a gun." A gun which, I fervently hoped, she could not be sure was empty. Of course, if she had kept a better count of the shots than I had—

"Lisa! Please! Don't go near that house."

"Mother, listen to me. It's not as if we could stay up here all night, risking nothing worse than pneumonia. When they don't find us anywhere between the house and the village, they'll start looking in the other direction. And they'll think of this hut. Don't you see?"

After a while she said in a subdued voice, "Be careful, darling."

I squeezed her shoulder. "I will."

I left the hut. The rain had slackened to a drizzle. The darkness was no longer complete, but relieved by a faint luminescence, as if the moon, which I knew must be nearing its last quarter, was now veiled by only a thin overcast. I struck off at an angle which I hoped would lead me to the old cedar. Soon I could make out its twisted shape. Despite the heavy mud on my boots and the way I seemed to sink several inches at each step, I tried to quicken my pace. The rain had increased again. Evidently the storm was tapering off into a series of intermittent showers.

A few feet short of the cedar I stopped, took off my white raincoat, and dropped it to the ground. Then, sure that in my dark skirt and sweater I would be invisible to anyone watching from below, I moved to the moor's edge.

No lights shone from the rear of Deveron Hall's dark bulk. And there seemed to be no sound anywhere except that of the rain and the dying wind. Just the same, I was determined to take no unnecessary chances. With my feet threatening to slide out from under me at every step, I descended the steep path.

The garage door was up. After a moment I stepped inside. The Buick was gone, but I could make out the old Bentley over in the corner, a deeper dark in the darkness. With the faint hope that I might find it unlocked, with its keys in the dashboard, I walked over and tried the door handle. Locked.

I started moving, as quietly as I could, across the gravel toward the kitchen door. Then I turned around. Now that I was almost certain that the house was empty, it would be best to go back to get my raincoat, so that I could carry the gun and yet have both hands free.

About five minutes later, wearing the raincoat, I again moved across the gravel to the house's rear entrance. The screen door was locked. So, presumably, was the solid door beyond. Then I was sure that they had gone, making it difficult for us, if we were driven to seek shelter from the storm, to get into the house and hide someplace. Perhaps, too, they had realized I might try to use the telephone.

I moved to a window. Sure that it was locked, I did not even try to slide the sash up. With the gun butt, I struck the lower pane and heard shattered glass fall to the kitchen floor. After dropping the gun back into my pocket, I wrapped my rain-sodden scarf around my wrist, reached cautiously through the opening in the glass, and turned the latch. When I had pushed at the top of the sash for several seconds, the pane slid up a few inches. I hooked my fingers beneath it and forced it the rest of the way up. Then I climbed inside.

Utter darkness here. And crossing the room at this angle, I would be sure to encounter furniture. Hands outstretched, I groped my way across the kitchen, touching and then moving around the table, and after that a chair. When I reached the far wall, it took me about a minute, moving first to my right and then to my left, to find the doorway, but at last I did. I moved along the short passage to the baize door and pushed it open.

At the hall's front end, enough faint light fell through the glass doors to show me the phone on its table. Heart beating fast and triumphantly, I lifted the phone to my ear.

Disappointment struck me like a physical blow. No humming tone. They had ripped out the wire before they left. Now I realized that I should have known they might have.

I dropped the useless instrument into its cradle and then looked at the dimly visible stairs. Try the extension? No, they would have ripped out the wire there, too. Best to get out of here while I still could.

Then my whole body tightened up. From the direction of the road came the sound of an engine laboring up the long muddy drive.

I ran. Back along the hall, through the baize door, along

the shorter passage to the kitchen. I should have stopped running then, but I did not, and I collided with the side of a chair and went over with it, striking my forehead against the linoleum.

I lay there for what must have been more than a minute, half stunned and with the breath knocked out of me. Then I got to my feet. I could see the pale rectangle of the open window now. I still had time, I told myself, as I moved toward it. Surely they had not been far up the drive when I heard their engine.

But as I swung my legs over the sill, I realized that Richard Coventry was driving much faster this time. The car sounded close, terribly close. I dropped to the ground, skirted the corner of the garage, started to climb the path. A swift glance upward showed me that headlights shone faintly on the cedar tree. But I could make it to the top before the car reached the level ground on which the house sat, and the lights swept down on me. Surely I could. Feet slipping, lungs straining, hands clutching at heather and gorse, I struggled upward. The Buick was moving even faster now.

Then the whole hillside was bathed in glare, and I knew with despairing terror that long before I reached the top a bullet could come crashing into my back.

The car had stopped. In another instant I would hear its door open. Feet slipping, I managed to turn around on the muddy path. Eyes dazzled by the glare, knowing it was useless and yet unable to think of anything else to do, I took the gun from my pocket and pointed it towards those headlights.

"Lisa!"

At almost the same instant that I heard his voice, I realized that those were not the Buick's headlights, not set that far above the ground. I cried, "Turn off the lights!"

The lights went out. In what seemed to me pitch blackness, and with my feet almost sliding from under me, I came the rest of the way down the path and into his arms.

Chapter Twenty

Michael said, "Oh, God! I knew I shouldn't have left you here. That's why I— What is it, Lisa. What is it?"

I clung to him, gasping for breath and wondering how to make him understand quickly. "You were right about her," I said. "She's a killer. She killed my father. She told me so." My words came faster. "And now she and that man are out looking for my mother and me—"

"But you just said your mother— Lisa, Lisa! Try to make sense."

I drew a deep breath. "She's not my mother, that woman that everyone up here thought was Marcia Deveron. She's my mother's Cousin Amy, and that man she brought here with her is her husband."

He was silent. I sensed he was putting it together. The discrepancy between Dr. Crandall's assessment of my mother and the viciousness he had seen in that woman's mirrored face that afternoon. The fact that the supposed "cousin" had not once been seen outside of Deveron Hall in all the weeks she had been here.

He said, "Were they after her money?"

"Yes."

He grasped my arm. "Let's get to the phone."

I said, holding back, "It's no use. They tore out the wires before they left."

He stood motionless for a moment and then said, "Give me that gun."

I handed it to him. "I'm afraid there are no bullets in it. And anyway, we've got to go get my mother. She's up on the moor in that hut, and her ankle's hurt."

Without answering, he strode to the Land Rover and opened its door. I heard the glove compartment creak open, saw the glow of a flashlight. Then he closed the car door and walked back to me. "The gun's empty. Where did you get it?"

"It's Amy's. I struggled with her, and the gun kept going off— But Michael! Didn't you hear me? We've got to get my mother and then drive away from here."

"I'm afraid it's too late for that. Coventry drives a blue Buick, doesn't he?"

I said from a suddenly dry throat, "Yes."

"I passed it on the way here. It was parked on the turnout about a mile on the other side of the bridge. There was a woman in the car and a man outside it wiping mud off the wind screen."

So again he was having trouble with the windshield wiper. "Do—do you think they knew who you were?"

"Probably. Anyway, they must have seen my headlights turn off the road to Deveron Hall. Do you know if they're armed?"

"No."

"They probably are. Anyway, they'll have followed me. They can't risk my finding out, or even guessing, that something is wrong here. They know I'd go to the constable, and that he'd call the police in Dingwall."

The distant whine of an engine. Headlights down there on the road, moving toward the foot of the drive.

I grasped his arm and said thinly, "Michael, we can't run and hide. They might go up on the moor and find—"

"I know. Get in the car."

Not asking questions, I moved with him to the Land Rover's dark bulk and climbed onto the high seat. He got in beside me. Without switching on the lights, he drove forward a few feet, backed onto the gravel between the garage and the house, and stopped.

"Listen carefully. We're going to drive a little way towards them without lights. Then we'll stop. I'll get out of the car. After that you're to count to five. Like this, one—two —and so on. Then you're to turn on the headlights. Here, give me your hand."

He guided my hand to the switch. "The instant you turn on the lights, duck down behind the dashboard. And stay down. No matter what you hear, *stay down.*"

My lips felt numb and clumsy. "Michael, if he has a gun—"

"So have I."

"But it's—"

"He won't know what gun it is, and he won't know it's empty."

Perhaps he wouldn't. And perhaps he would. I said, "If it works, what are you—"

"I'll hold them here. You'll go wake the constable. Let's go."

He started the car and drove around the corner of the house. Those distant headlights, two small yellowish circles, had already turned onto the drive. We moved toward them. Heart hammering, hands icy cold, I was only dimly aware of the rain's patter on the car roof, and of the tall black pines sliding past on either side of the drive.

The Buick's headlights appeared larger now. Despite the

light curtain of rain, soon their beam would touch the Land Rover's lightless bulk. Michael stopped. "Not until after you've counted five," he reminded me. "After that, keep down." He opened the door, got out, and closed it almost soundlessly. As I began to count, I was aware of him slipping out of sight beyond the line of trees at my right.

Heartbeats thunderous now, gaze riveted on those approaching lights, I finished the count. Then I turned the switch and fell sideways to the seat, bathed in the refracted glow of the Buick's and the Land Rover's mingled headlights.

The sound of the Buick's engine abruptly ceased. I heard Michael call out from somewhere down the road, "All right. I've got a gun pointed right at you. Both of you get out, with your hands up."

I had a terrifying vision of him standing close to a pine tree down there somewhere, that useless gun in his hand. Would it work, or would Coventry guess, from what Amy must have told him, that the gun was hers, and empty now? Breath held, I strained my ears for the sound of a car door opening.

Instead I heard a shot, then two more. Even if I had remembered Michael's injunction, and in my terror for him I did not, I still would have sat up.

Coventry's first shots, I saw, must have missed, because bathed by the Land Rover's headlights he was trotting down the drive beyond his own car, as if trying to get a clear shot at someone moving beyond the line of trees. I saw him lift his arm, fire.

Then a crouched figure hurtled into my line of vision. Coventry fired again, but Michael must have dived under the shot, because both men went down, there at the drive's edge.

Frozen, unable to move, I watched the two struggling figures roll over and over. I saw a raised arm and fist—whose I could not tell—deliver a blow. Then one of them got half-way to his feet. With a relief that left me almost nauseous, I recognized Michael's tall thin figure. I saw him lift Coventry by his collar and drive his fist once, and then again, at his jaw.

The Buick was backing away down the drive. So Amy, aware that Coventry could no longer help her, was going to make a run for it.

Michael was on his feet now. I saw him drag Coventry off into the shallow depression between the drive's edge and the line of trees. Then he returned to the drive and seemed to be searching for something on the muddy ground. Coventry's gun? It must be. So as to leave both hands free, he surely had dropped that empty gun before he launched himself at the other man.

I saw him stoop, pick something up. Then he was moving toward me along the muddy drive, slowly and unsteadily. When he was within a few hundred feet of the Land Rover I saw, heart contracting, that bright red blood was running down the right side of his face from a forehead cut. I reached for the door handle, swung the door open, and glanced back at Michael in time to see him slip in the mud and fall heavily to his side.

Then I sat motionless, paralyzed, Amy also had seen him fall. She had reversed the Buick and was moving forward. I screamed "Michael!" but I don't know whether it was my voice or the sound of the oncoming car that alerted him. He lifted himself to one elbow, fired one futile shot at those headlights. Then he was on his feet. I saw him take a step to the right, slip and fall again, and then lie motionless at the drive's edge.

With despair I realized that before I could reach him and drag him to safety, the Buick would have crushed him beneath its wheels. I slammed the car door, slid over on the seat, switched on the ignition. The Land Rover bucked slightly as I pressed on the accelerator, and then shot forward.

Those headlights were still coming. Even when I had passed Michael's still figure, they were still coming. But she would have to give way, that woman behind the wheel, that murderer of my father, that destroyer of my mother's life. The Land Rover was bigger, heavier. She would have to give way.

But she was still coming. I pictured her there in the driver's seat, lips stretched in a vicious little smile, grimly certain that I, daughter of that "soft-headed fool," would be the one to lose nerve and swerve off the drive to crash against a tree or boulder, leaving her free to deal with that fallen man back there.

I pressed harder on the accelerator. The Land Rover gathered speed.

We were within feet of each other when the Buick shot off the drive to the left. I heard a grinding crash.

Momentum carried the Land Rover forward a few yards even after I had lifted my foot from the accelerator. Then the engine coughed, and the car stopped. I slumped forward over the wheel, vision blurred, helpless under a wave of dizziness and nausea. I knew that if I tried to get out of the car I would faint.

I was still slumped there, trying to conquer that sick vertigo, when I heard Michael say, "Lisa! Are you all right?"

I risked sitting up. He stood beside the car, one hand holding a bloodied handkerchief to his forehead. I asked thinly, "How bad are you—"

"Not much. He managed to hit me with the gun barrel before he dropped it, and I was dazed for a while. But I'm all right now, and the bleeding has almost stopped." He added, "Just sit there for a few minutes, darling."

Perhaps as long as five minutes passed before he returned. I said, "That woman—"

"She's dead. Don't go over there. She hit a tree, and the steering column went right through— Just sit there for a while longer." He started to move toward the rear of the car.

"Michael—"

He turned back to me. "I'm going to get rope out of the trunk. Coventry's still out, and I want to make sure that by the time he comes to he will be tied up and helpless."

I asked, "And after that?" although I already knew the answer.

"I'll go up on the moor and get your mother. Do you think you can drive now?" I nodded.

"Then go down to the village, darling, and wake Constable MacNeil. His house is the one just this side of the pub. Hammer on the door as hard as you can. He's quite deaf."

Chapter
Twenty-one

Even though it was still not quite September, the night air
out on the terrace above the loch was cool, so much so that I
wore a knitted white shawl over my sleeveless blue dinner
dress. The shawl, once the property of Michael's grandmother, had been a pre-nuptial gift from James MacKelvin.

Michael said, smiling down at me, "Well, has it been decided? Will it be a buffet, or just maids handing things
around on trays?"

He meant for the wedding reception at Deveron Hall.
"Just trays." I looked up at him, thinking not of the reception but of our wedding trip afterward. We were not going
to Paris, or the Greek islands, or any of the usual places. Instead Michael had already reserved in Inverness a vehicle
that I called a camper and he called a caravan. In it we
would drive all over Scotland. And on mild nights we would
spread out our air mattress beside it, under the stars.

"What made you decide on trays?"

"That Inverness caterer agrees with Mother and me. A
buffet would be too much. After all, the whole village will
be there."

Or at least most of it. Jennie Graham, who weeks before
had been replaced by a live-in couple from Dingwall, was
not invited, nor was her "distant cousin" Johnny. And knowing they would not come in any case, we had not asked

those two elderly Grahams up in their narrow glen. But otherwise every villager over the age of twelve had been invited to the kirk for the ceremony, and to Deveron Hall afterward.

"When I picked you up tonight," Michael said, "I noticed how pretty your mother has become."

I nodded. She had put on several pounds these past weeks, and her green-eyed face in its frame of gray curls had regained much of the soft animation I remembered from my childhood.

"She's a remarkable woman," Michael said. "Almost anyone else would be in London or someplace now, leaving Deveron Hall up for sale."

I looked down at the loch, dark and mirror-smooth under the light of a first-quarter moon. "She was born there, Michael. Besides, after all those lonely years, she wants to be near me—near us."

"Yes, I know. And apparently she's like a lot of gentle people. She has a vein of iron underneath. Look at how well she has stood up under everything."

I knew what he meant by everything. He meant the inquest in Dingwall into Amy Coventry's death, when my mother had listened, pale but calm, while Michael and I described the events of that storm-lashed night. He meant Richard Coventry's preliminary hearing on charges of attempted murder and conspiracy to commit grand theft, when she had added her testimony to Michael's and mine—testimony that would hold Coventry behind bars for an indeterminate number of years.

There has been the reporters too, flocking up from London and Edinburgh and Glasgow to the inquest, and later on to Richard Coventry's preliminary hearing and trial. But the G 47 reporters were gone now, and this part of the Highlands was left to its isolation and peace.

Something had broken the loch's smooth surface—a dark, moving object that left a rippling wake. I said, "Look. At long last, there's your monster."

After a moment he said, "It's an otter. There's no monster, I'm afraid."

I thought of the day when I had sat on the bench outside the village garage, and looked across the valley, and felt a sense of some monstrous evil moving beneath the beautiful surface of things. Unlike Michael's monster, that evil had been real. But it was vanquished now. "No," I said, "no monster."

He smiled down at me. "Perhaps we'd better go in, darling. We promised my father a game of backgammon, remember."

I looked again at the little creature, arrowing through the dark water. Then Michael and I, with his arm around me, went into the house.